Frankie's Journey

Leah Brewer

In memory of my late grandma, Frances Cornela Little Owens, also known as Frankie. You kept me on my toes!

Author's Note

Nearly three years ago, I embarked on a deeply personal mission to bring the first installment of this series, Keatyn's Journey, to life.

Since the release of this series, I have faced the painful reality of losing my beloved cover model from Keatyn's Journey, Samantha. She was a radiant spirit whose light shone brightly, bringing joy to everyone around her. I cherished her deeply, and her absence is profoundly felt every day by all who loved her.

In her honor, I made the decision to revisit and revise the books in this series to make them the best they can be.

Thank you to everyone who took the time to read and review the books. Your insightful comments have been invaluable in shaping these revisions. May God bless you all!

Chapter 1

Despite the relentless cold rain that drenched their clothes, Frankie Kingston and Melody Rodgers huddled together on the rough, stony bench outside their old high school.

Who better to contemplate the mysteries of life with than your best friend? Frankie, with her fair skin and a cascade of curly dark hair that seemed to bounce with every step, exuded a vibrant energy that drew people in. In contrast, Melody, with her beautifully bronzed complexion and sleek, straight dark hair that shimmered in the sunlight, radiated a calm and soothing presence. Despite their differences, their bond had been unbreakable since their youth.

The scent of wet earth filled the air as dark clouds loomed overhead, casting a gloomy shadow over the small town of Des Arc, Arkansas. Thunder rumbled in the distance, punctuated by brilliant flashes of lightning that illuminated the horizon. Frankie's heart raced as she silently prayed that the approaching storm would shift, staying closer to Hazen and sparing Des Arc from its fury.

A strand of Frankie's hair fell onto the bench. She picked it up, the wind caught it, and it floated away. Her gaze stayed glued to that lone hair strand until it disappeared. She couldn't help but compare it to Daddy. Just like the hair, he had left her behind. She could do nothing to change it, like fighting against the wind.

Frankie dropped her head a second before raising it to stare at the proud eagle close to the road. "I'm not even twenty-four years old, and I'm all alone."

Melody hugged Frankie close, careful to keep the umbrella from falling. "You'll never be alone as long as I'm alive."

Frankie smiled, warmth flooding her heart as she looked at Melody. "Thank you for being here for me."

"Always." Melody held her hand out, raindrops glistening on her skin. "Come on, let's get you into some dry clothes. It's already after one."

Frankie bolted off the bench. "I need to go see Daddy's attorney. I'm late."

After a quick shower and change of clothes, Frankie eyeballed Simon Wheeler. "Daddy did what?" Frankie's stomach dropped. "Did you say he bought a camp for orphans?"

She never dreamed that the meeting with Daddy's attorney would be like this. Why would he leave his only daughter with a burden of such magnitude on top of dealing with his death?

Glancing around the room, Frankie attempted to keep a neutral expression. The only thing that helped was focusing on a painting of an old barn surrounded by rolling hills hanging behind the attorney.

Simon patted her hand—the turquoise ring shaped like a bird brought Frankie's attention to his index finger. Simon had always been a quirky man, but Daddy touted him as the best attorney in the state. "Not specifically for them, but to help give them a purpose during the holidays. You know he always had a soft spot for the Children's Home there in Pensacola."

"Yes, I know." She steadily shook her head. "Daddy did, but that has nothing to do with me."

Simon cocked his head, and a piece of graying hair fell into his face. He smoothed it back into place and creased his forehead. "It may not have then, but it does now."

Jerking her gaze from the painting, she stared head-on at Simon. "Why do you say that?"

Simon swiveled his light orange leather chair around and clicked a button on the TV screen. "I think it'll be better for you to hear it from Larry."

Daddy appeared on the screen with a head full of dark hair and color on his face. He must've made the video soon after his cancer diagnosis. His brown eyes implored her to listen from the screen.

"Hello, my dear Frances. I hope you understand my intentions. Pensacola has always held a special place in my heart, and as someone who was once an orphan until I was adopted, I feel a deep desire to help the children at the Pensacola Children's Home who are still waiting for families. That's why I purchased the camp. I envisioned transforming it into a haven for joy and creativity. I even began renovations before I fell ill. Frances, I'm asking you to carry on this mission. Organize a Christmas Festival where the kids can run booths and truly engage with the spirit of the season. They deserve an outlet for positivity and connection. I regret not sharing this with you sooner, especially since I know Christmas has been challenging for you. I had hoped to bring you to the camp myself. I believe in your ability to bring happiness to those kids, and I know it will also rejuvenate your spirit. You have the biggest heart. Please go to the house in Pensacola and do your best for them. And cherish my car—drive it joyfully and think of the smiles it brings me to envision you behind the wheel. I love you dearly; you are my pride and joy. Lastly, I hope you embrace love for the Lord fully. I look

forward to the day we reunite in Heaven. Until then, take care of yourself."

Frankie sat stunned for a few minutes, letting what Daddy said sink in.

Simon cleared his throat. "Listen, I know this is a lot to take in. Do you need some time to think about it?"

Itching to peel off all her fingernails, she stuffed both hands underneath her legs to avoid leaving the office with nubs. How could Daddy ask her to do such a thing? "So, what happens if I say no? Do I sell the property?"

Smoothing the papers on his desk, Simon's voice came out steady and firm. "Not exactly. Suppose you decline to take the property on, as your father requested. In that case, it will be given to the second person in line."

Frankie cocked her head and screwed her lips up. "Who is that?"

Simon shrugged. "I'm not at liberty to discuss that just yet, but you'll still get your inheritance on top of his life insurance."

Frankie's brow furrowed. "That's not what it's about. I'm not worried about money, Simon. Who else could Daddy have left something to? We don't have any family left."

Simon shrugged again but didn't say anything. Silence closed in on them while Frankie pondered her next move. Daddy had always taught her to think before speaking, especially when upset.

She leaned forward, attempting to see if she could see any other names in the papers. Simon raised a brow as he stacked the papers and slipped them inside his briefcase. She inwardly groaned. Simon might be pushing seventy-something, but he was still alert as ever. "Can I stop by in the morning? That'll give me time to think about what I want to do."

He laid the briefcase on the desk, almost daring her to grab it. "What's your first inclination?"

She tore her gaze away from the briefcase and met his eyes. "Honestly, as bad as I want to run out of this office and never look back, I can't. I probably should move to Pensacola and do what Daddy asked. For him. But Arkansas is my home, not Florida."

"I've been your daddy's friend for over thirty years, and I know he asked you to do this for a reason. Maybe you should listen to your heart and not your head."

Yeah, if only Frankie liked kids.

Chapter 2

Frankie skidded a rock into Lake Des Arc. "Why would Daddy force this on me? He knows I don't celebrate Christmas." She pinched her eyes closed as a shot of loss hit her body and soul. "Or knew, rather."

Melody gathered a handful of rocks before looking at Frankie with a sad expression. "We may never know what made him do this. But I have faith he did it for a reason."

Throwing another rock as far as possible, Frankie's lips pulled into a frown. "I have to wonder. Especially since he's taking me away from my best friend and a job I love."

Melody zipped her sweater and shivered. "This will just give me a reason to finally go to the beach there."

"True." Frankie stared at the sky as a few sun rays shone behind a puffy white cloud. "But I think Brayden is on the verge of finally asking me out."

A lizard skittered by Melody's foot, entering the water. Melody focused on the spot where the lizard disappeared before looking at Frankie with a sigh. "He's had plenty of time to ask you out. I didn't want to tell you this, but he went out with Emily last night."

Frankie's mind whirled. How could he choose to date Emily over her? Florida looked better and better. The only bad thing was if she moved, she'd have to start all over. "I can't leave my job, though. They need me there."

Melody raised a brow and cocked her head. Oh no. The look. Ever since they'd met when they were both thirteen, Melody had always been able to make Frankie feel bad for things she'd either said or done. With just a look. It had gotten worse after Mama passed away. It was like Melody felt the need to take over as Frankie's surrogate mama. A single father had raised Melody and her little brother, so maybe Melody's *"Mom Stare"* came naturally.

A couple of fishermen loaded a boat in the water, and within a few minutes, the motor roared to life. They waved as they buzzed by, heading for deeper water.

As the humming motor got lower and lower, Frankie screwed her lips up and linked her arm with Melody's. "Come on, Mama dear. I have to work this afternoon."

Melody grinned. "Mama has a nice ring to it."

Frankie's head whipped around, and she came to a halt. "Are you pregnant?"

Melody bit her bottom lip and grinned. "Not yet, but Raines and I decided it's time to start a family."

All worries left Frankie's mind as she let out a squeal. "Now I know I can't move to Florida. My best friend's gonna have a baby."

Melody shook her head as her grin expanded. "I said we decided to try, silly. I'm not pregnant yet."

"Well, I don't want to miss it." The grin dissolved into a frown as Frankie's stomach churned. "I can't move."

"Yes, you can." Melody's blue-gray eyes widened as she met Frankie's gaze. Those same blue-gray eyes were what started their friendship. When Melody moved to Des Arc, Frankie had asked if she wore colored contacts. Melody had laughed and said nope, that she was unique with her darker skin and lighter eyes. Frankie had agreed, and they hung out at the Dairy Bar after school that same day.

Melody's voice interrupted Frankie's memory. "This is what your daddy wanted. I promise I'll be visiting you in Florida all the time. And you can come back here as often as you want to."

"I'm not selling the house here, so I guess you're right." Frankie's churning stomach could have made a bucket of butter. She pressed her abdomen and groaned. "All this talk of moving is making my stomach hurt."

An hour later, Frankie pushed the door to The Lily Pad Boutique open. Angie looked up from a rack of clothes. "Hey. How are you doing this afternoon?"

Shivers racked Frankie's spine. She ignored them by putting a big smile on her face and diving into organizing the sales floor.

Chapter 3

By the time April changed to May, Frankie had most of her things packed for Florida. She put the last suitcase in the trunk of Daddy's Camaro and sighed. She'd always teased him about taking this car away but never wanted to have it this way.

Before he got too sick, he'd spend hours waxing the glossy white paint and take extra care when he got to the red stripes that ran down the hood and trunk. He kept the white convertible top and red leather seats looking like new. Frankie had sometimes wondered if he loved that car more than her. But she knew that was a ridiculous notion.

She let her eyes take in one last look at the home she'd lived in for over half her life before shutting the trunk. "Welp, that's the last of it. I'm officially ready to leave Arkansas behind and move to Florida. Well, not ready ready. Just packed."

Raines Rodgers leaned by the rear tire and checked the tire pressure. He used the side of the car to pull himself off the ground. He ran a hand through his light brown locks. "Yep, you sure are. Tires all look good."

Wrapping her hands around Melody, Frankie groaned. "Ugh. Y'all, please move to Florida with me."

"Hey. I'm down for that." She elbowed Raines. "But we would have to talk this one into it. And we'd need jobs."

Frankie's eyes lit up. "There's a hospital in Pensacola. Y'all can work there."

Raines shook his head. "I doubt they're looking for two ER nurses. We lucked out when the hospital at Searcy hired us both."

"But what if they are?" Frankie pooched her bottom lip out. "Will you at least think about it?"

Melody swiped her fingers down Frankie's lip. "Maybe."

Frankie clapped her hands together. "That's better than a no." A serious expression crossed her features. "Hey, I can't tell you how much I appreciate you both taking time off work to help me move."

"No thanks needed. We'd do anything for you," Melody commented.

"I second that. Now you just make sure you're careful driving." Raines pecked Melody on the lips. "I'll be right behind y'all as long as Speedy doesn't try to go off and leave me."

Melody grinned. "I'll make sure she doesn't. Love you, babe."

"Love you, too." He waved as he buckled the seatbelt in Frankie's inherited Tahoe.

Frankie had considered leaving it behind but decided she might need it for the kids. She wasn't sure what would happen or what she might need. And it would be better to be prepared for any possibility.

Nine hours later, Melody stepped out of the Camaro and gasped at the historic two-story house. "Um, Frankie? I'll talk Raines into moving if we can live here with you."

Raines sidled up beside Melody and set a suitcase on the ground. "This place is massive."

Frankie took in the home she still considered her grandparents' as she made her way up the steps. White columns flanked three wide steps that led to the light-blue door. The porch boasted a white swing filled with teal and peach pillows on the right side and two matching white rocking chairs with a small table in between on the left. Frankie remembered sitting on the porch for hours on end, waiting for the next-door neighbor's son to make an appearance.

"I spent many summers here as a kid." She paused, her hand hovering above the front porch railing, and glanced back at Melody and Raines with a half-smile. "I loved making up ghost stories and scaring myself to death."

The front door opened, and a gray-haired woman stepped outside. Frankie jumped and slapped her right hand above her heart. "Oh, my goodness."

"Oh dear," the woman said as she pulled her light blue granny gown away from her belly. "I've scared you, poor thing. I sure didn't mean to."

Frankie swallowed down the scream, threatening to blast out. "Who are you?"

"I'm Vandon Wilcox, dear. Your daddy must've told you I'd be here." Her round face crinkled all over when she smiled. "Don't you remember me?"

"Um, hello, yes." Frankie blinked a few times. Vandon reminded her of Rose from that show about the older women living together in Miami, but with a slight pudge around the middle. Frankie's mind raced as she tried to remember the name of the show. Oh well, Vandon must be the one Daddy said would be here to help.

Raines and Melody skipped up the steps to stand beside Frankie. "These are my friends, Melody and her husband, Raines."

Vandon moved to the side of the door and put her hand out. "Come in, please. Can I get you all anything to eat or drink?"

Frankie stepped through the double front doors, and her eyes darted from the living room to the open kitchen. The living room held the longest white sectional sofa she'd ever seen with a matching ottoman and zebra rug. Two additional seating areas were scattered around the room. One with two white and yellow zebra print wingback chairs and the other with two navy wingback chairs identical to the zebra print ones.

The open kitchen had an island with six navy barstools, a white table with six chairs sporting yellow zebra print cushions, and top-of-the-line stainless steel appliances. The exposed brick wall brought back a memory of the day she opened Grandma's French cabinet and pulled her set of antique China out. She'd set up tea for two on the table and even poured some into the glasses. Grandma about had a stroke when she walked in, but Grandpa had chuckled and told Grandma to leave her alone.

After letting the memories flow for a minute, she found her voice. "No, thank you. We just want to get some sleep."

Vandon's eyes glistened. "Your daddy hoped you'd be pleased with his chosen decorations."

Her grandparents had remodeled the historic home to give it an open concept. She should've known Daddy would update it to suit her tastes. Frankie's expression softened, and she lifted her lips. "I am. Very much so. Thank you."

Vandon grinned. "Perfect. Now, you three follow me. I'll show you to your rooms."

Chapter 4

Alex Foster closed the hood on his Black Chevy Silverado and wiped his oily hands on a towel. He'd finally done it. He'd transitioned from CPA to small business owner of Foster's Lawn and Landscaping.

He couldn't wait to get his hands dirty.

It turned out he didn't enjoy all the busy bookwork like his dad, Alex Sr. He'd earned his money growing up by mowing yards, and he'd much rather dig in the dirt than dig through numbers. His next-door neighbors, the Kingston's, had gotten him started on the path when he was twelve by offering him twenty bucks a week to mow for them.

After mowing a few months, he'd gone from the scrawny, redheaded nerd to a slightly more buff, redheaded nerd. But the girls paid him a lot more attention, at least.

He blew a low whistle when an old-school Camaro pulled into the Kingston driveway. It had to be Larry's. He'd told Alex he had bought one a few years back, but if that was it, Alex hadn't expected it to look like that.

He sucked in a breath when a woman with long dark hair emerged from the vehicle. The light from a Tahoe pulling into the driveway hit her face, and Alex almost ducked behind his truck.

Little Frankie Kingston didn't look so little anymore.

Seeing her caused his mind to drift back almost ten years to a talkative girl with dark fuzzy curls following him around, trying to get him to let her mow. He'd always thought it was cute until she'd hit her teen years.

After she became a little flirtatious, he'd tried to set her straight on more than one occasion. He was not interested in going to jail for anyone. She was a sweet girl that he thought a lot of, but not for him. Not like that anyway.

He'd managed to avoid being alone with her most of the summer after graduation until she showed up at the front door. If she'd waited ten minutes longer, he would've been on the way to Mississippi State and missed her visit.

"Alex. Frankie's here to say goodbye," Mom had yelled up the stairs.

He cringed with the next memory.

"Hi, Frankie," he'd said as Mom walked out of the room. Maybe they could leave on good terms. He'd always had a soft spot for her and hoped she understood why they couldn't be more than friends. He remembered the utter shock that had rocked his body when Frankie walked up to him, planting a kiss on his mouth.

Mom chose that moment to walk back into the living room. "ALEX! What are you doing, son? Frankie is way too young for you."

His heart dropped as he watched Frankie's eyes fill with horrified tears. Her lips trembled as she landed a look of pure love on Alex before sprinting through the front door. He'd wanted to burst into tears himself as Mom proceeded to chew him out. She'd even called Dad into the room so he could also chew him out.

After dinner, Frankie's father and grandfather came over for a talk. Larry Kingston had been upset and even demanded to know what Alex had done, but William Kingston had patted his knee and told them he knew what happened had been all Frankie's doing. Apparently, Frankie confessed what she did. After hearing that, Larry's attitude changed to apologetic, and he promised to ensure Frankie stayed far away from Alex the following summer.

After William and Larry left, Alex climbed into his Nissan Altima, and a piece of paper was lying in his front passenger's seat. The only two words on it were *I'm sorry.*

Chapter 5

P edro's Pizza was reasonably busy, with half of their tables filled. The mouthwatering scent of fresh pizza and breadsticks surrounded Frankie, and her stomach growled.

The Spanish tune playing in the background was almost drowned out by a table of college students laughing and carrying on. One of the college students stared at Frankie and kept saying, "Hey, girl."

Frankie ignored him and let the cool air hit her face. "Ah, this feels good."

"Frankie?" A chunky woman sauntered up to Frankie's table. That's all it took for the young college student to return his attention to his friends.

Frankie's lips curved into a smile as she focused on her late grandma's best friend. "Hi, Aunt Cordelia."

Cordelia stepped aside, giving the waitress room to put a pizza on their table. "When did you get back in town?"

"We drove in late last night." Frankie thanked the waitress before putting her attention back on Cordelia. "This is Raines and Melody Rodgers."

"Hello." Laugh lines crinkled around her eyes and mouth as she smiled at them before bestowing a sympathetic frown on Frankie. "I was so sorry to hear about Larry's passing. And I was just sick I couldn't be there for you in person. Myles had the flu, and I dared not leave him."

"I know. I appreciate the calls and the cards." Frankie cleared her throat, swallowing the emotion. "They helped more than you know."

Cordelia put her arms up. "Come here and give me a hug."

Frankie rose out of her chair and stepped into Cordelia's warm arms. She inhaled sweet Snicker-doodle cookies before taking her seat. "Did you hear about what Daddy did?"

Cordelia's gaze bounced to the front door as she answered Frankie, "Which part, honey? The cabins?"

A burn bordered the corners of Frankie's eyes. "I guess." She could be such a crybaby sometimes.

"I heard." She shifted her light gray purse from her left shoulder to her right. "And I'll tell you, that camp will be a lifesaver to many kids who don't have much to look forward to around Christmas."

"I imagine." Frankie's eyes took stock of the pizza, and her stomach made another gurgle. "It's a good thing. I'm just worried about how much time it'll take to remodel the cabins."

Cordelia nodded and looked toward the entrance again. "They need some work, but you have time to make it happen before December."

"So, you know about the stipulation in his will? Making me turn that place into a Christmas camp or else?" Her throat lurched as she swallowed the tears that continued to threaten her.

"I do know, and don't you worry. There are plenty of people from the congregation ready to help."

A tall, gray-haired man entered the restaurant and limped over to their table using a cane.

Cordelia continued, "This is my dear husband, Myles, and we'd love to help, but we'll be in India for the next few months."

After a brief introduction, Frankie motioned to the two empty seats. "You are both welcome to join us for lunch. I'd like to hear about your trip."

"We'd love to," Myles said.

About halfway through their meal, Cordelia pinned Frankie with her eyes. "I do hope you're planning to be in service Sunday. We're leaving Monday morning, and I want to see you before we go."

Swallowing the bite of pineapple and pepperoni pizza, Frankie washed it down with a swig of lemon water. "I've kinda gotten used to attending online. You know, with staying home taking care of Daddy."

"Larry would want you back in service."

Darting her eyes to Melody, wordlessly begging her to save her, Frankie laughed. "I'll try." Cordelia didn't need to know Frankie had no intention of returning to church—at least not right this second.

"What about you two?" Myles interjected.

Melody ignored Frankie's pleading expression. "Raines and I would love to come."

Shooting Melody a dirty look before pasting a pinched smile on for Cordelia, Frankie settled her arms across her chest. "Guess that means we'll be there."

"Oh, goody." Laugh lines creased around Cordelia's eyes. "I'll look for all three of y'all at nine Sunday morning."

Chapter 6

The camp Daddy had purchased sat on six acres far north of Pensacola. It only took Frankie fifteen minutes to get to the turnoff from Pedro's Pizza.

As they made their way down the road, the beauty of the trees and sky struck Frankie's eyes and heart. At least Daddy bought a scenic place.

After driving for five minutes, they came to a roundabout with three ways to go. The first sign said Loblolly Lake, the second said Barn and the third said Cabins.

She clicked the blinker to turn down the road labeled Cabins, and Melody giggled. Frankie eyed her and let out a laugh of her own. "Yeah, I used my blinker. Out in the middle of nowhere. What are you laughing at? I'm simply obeying the law."

"Mmmhmm. What's funny is how I've never noticed you using your blinker in Arkansas."

"Me neither," Raines piped in.

"Okay, y'all, leave me alone." She stuck her tongue out.

They came upon ten small log cabins about ten feet between them and a larger cabin around fifty feet from the nearest small cabin. The main cabin had a circle drive and extra space for parking on the right side. A black Chevy Silverado sat in front of the cabin.

"Lookee lookee." Melody motioned toward the cabins. "Does the truck come with the cabins, or is someone here?"

"Guess we'll find out," Raines said as he hopped out of the back seat with Melody and Frankie not far behind. "Frankie, this is a perfect space."

Frankie scanned her surroundings, her eyes landing on a giant fire pit and an area with a ratty soccer net. A snippet of the lake stood out in between the trees. "It seems to have potential, at least."

"Yeah, better to look at the positive," Melody replied.

Digging a key chain out of her pocket, Frankie sighed and tossed them to Raines. "Let's start at the main cabin, and then, we can see what I'm working with on the rest."

Raines unlocked the door and stepped inside. Frankie groaned as she walked in. From the looks of it, the place had been abandoned for years.

Brown paneling covered every wall; most had strips torn out from nails or tape. The carpet looked like, at one time, it had been a putrid yellow. Stains from a leak in the ceiling added a bit of brown on top of the yellow. The kitchen seemed lost in the seventies. The only bright spot was a room at the far back of the cabin. Frankie decided it would make a good game room for the kids.

Melody followed Raines out the large sliding glass door as Frankie walked down the long hallway. She kept her hand on the taser she kept on her key ring. Daddy had given her a flashlight with a hidden weapon when she first left for college. So far, she'd never used it but was ready to if needed.

A noise sounded from the first room on the left. She looked back to call for Raines, but he and Melody were already out of sight.

No matter, she could take care of herself.

She better get used to it now that she had no family left.

Easing the door open, she walked into the room with her flashlight taser raised and her finger on the button. A man stood in the middle of the room with his back to her, clearly holding a weapon.

She wasted no time slamming the taser into the man's neck.

The man let out a welp and dropped to his knees. By that time, Raines and Melody had come into the room. "Frankie, what's going on?"

Frankie jerked the taser back and backstepped close to where they stood. "We have an intruder."

The intruder slowly pushed himself to stand. He whirled about, and Frankie let out a gasp. Intoxicating yet livid green eyes skewered Frankie.

Oh no. Alex Foster.

Why did it have to be him, of all people? And why did he have to be drop-dead gorgeous? Why couldn't he be one of those boys who are super cute as teenagers but grow up to be unattractive?

Because Frankie could never get that lucky.

He laid the weapon er, screwdriver, on the windowsill, pulled a pair of earbuds out of his ears, and dropped them on the dirty brown shag carpet.

"I should've known it was you." He spoke through lips that seemed pressed so tight you couldn't even wedge a piece of paper between them.

"I'm so sorry, Alex." The heat coming from her neck told her either a pink or blood-red sheen stained her neck and ears. "I thought you were an intruder."

Melody's head jerked toward Frankie, and her eyebrows jutted so high they almost blended with her brown bangs. "Did you just call him Alex?"

"Yes," Frankie squeaked.

"*The* Alex?"

"Yes, my name is Alex." He rubbed the back of his neck and winced before leaning on the wall. "I can't believe you tased me."

Heat continued to lather her skin, and her insides trembled. "Like I said, I didn't know it was you."

His nostrils flared as he took a step toward Frankie. "And you didn't think to ask questions before trying to harm someone?"

Her thumb rubbed the power button on the taser as she backed away from Alex. "What are you doing on my property anyway?"

His mouth clenched as he picked up the earbuds. "Your property?"

Swallowing her emotion, she tried to ignore the embarrassment threatening to overtake her body. She had a strong urge to run out the door. "Yes. Daddy bought this place."

"Yeah, I know. I was there. This is our property." His tone came out low, like he fought the urge to throttle her.

"Um, no. Daddy left this place to me." Frankie's face contorted into a scowl. Let him try something. She'd happily pop him with the taser again. "Not you."

"Um, yeah. He left you the half he owned. I own the other half." The side of his mouth quirked up as a fake smile landed on Frankie. "We're partners."

Partners?!? She could not be partners with Alex Foster. Not after everything that happened – she'd die of mortification first.

She turned on her heel and stomped through the door. Before she made it another step, she stopped, swiveled her body, and met Alex's shocked gaze. "We'll see about that."

Chapter 7

A steady buzzing sounded from Frankie's bedside table. She rolled over and grabbed her phone. "Good morning, Simon. Thanks for returning my call."

"Morning, Frankie. How can I help you?"

She smacked her tongue against the roof of her mouth and grimaced. After going to the bathroom, she hit the mute button and swished a swig of mint mouthwash around her mouth.

She rid herself of the mouthwash and turned the speaker back on. "What do we have to do to buy Alex Foster out of his part of the cabins?"

"Unfortunately, it's not quite that simple."

Her jaw tightened as she walked into her bedroom. "Why not?"

"Frankie, I'm sorry, but I have to put you on hold for a minute."

"Okay." Before leaving the house, she pulled on a pair of black running shorts, a T-shirt, and tennis shoes.

Heading in the opposite direction of Alex's, she sighed. She couldn't believe he still lived in Pensacola. After ten years, she never would've dreamed he could still make her heart rev into high gear like no one else had before or after him. Her feelings had been a childhood crush, so why couldn't she get him off her mind?

She had to stop herself from grinning when she thought about her actions the day before. Smiling about tasing someone was not nice.

Even if that someone deserved it.

Was it normal to tase someone? No, she was at fault. But he should've been paying attention to what he was doing.

Would things ever get back to normal in her life? That was a stupid question. With Daddy gone, what even was normal? Being alone?

At least she had Vandon to keep her company after Raines and Melody returned to Arkansas. A woman she didn't even know, but Daddy trusted her, so that was good enough for Frankie.

Simon's voice interrupted her thoughts. "I'm sorry, but I spoke with Mr. Foster yesterday after hearing your message. He's not interested in selling."

Her stomach dropped. Yes, he'd deserved that tasing. "I appreciate you for trying. I'll speak to him as well. And if he won't sell to me, then maybe I should sell to him."

"Remember, Larry's will stipulates you are to oversee the festival. If you choose not to, the property reverts to the next in line."

They said their goodbyes as Frankie continued her run. She didn't even care who the second in line was. Common sense told her it had to be Alex, though.

An hour later, she slammed through the front door and entered the kitchen. Alex would inherit the property for nothing if he chose not to sell. Could she allow that to happen? Who was he to Daddy anyway?

On the other hand, owning the cabins with Alex would never work. She couldn't do it. There's no way she'd be able to see his face all the time. Her heart couldn't take it. He had to sell. Or she'd sign her half over and just let him inherit it.

She grabbed a strawberry toaster strudel out of the freezer. Kicking the drawer closed, she popped the strudel in the toaster.

Vandon walked into the kitchen with Melody close behind. "What are you doing making all this racket?" She stared at Frankie before pouring a cup of black coffee.

Frankie's hand landed on her chest. "Oh, Vandon, Melody, I'm sorry."

Melody plopped on a stool and grabbed a handful of pecans from a jar. "What's happened?"

"Simon told me that there's nothing I can do. Alex owns half the cabins." The strudel popped up, and

Frankie pushed it down again. "I can't believe this is happening."

After jiggling her eyebrows, Melody snickered. "This may be a good thing. That man is a looker."

The toaster popped the strudel out, and this time it was burned. Frankie grabbed it and put it on her plate. Then burst into tears.

Melody hopped up and hugged Frankie. "It's gonna be okay."

Frankie's mouth set into a determined line. "You know what? You're right. I'll figure out a way to make that man sell or I'll give him my half." She threw the burned toaster strudel in the trash and grabbed the box from the freezer. "Now, who wants a toaster strudel?"

Melody raised her hand. "I'll take one if it's strawberry."

Frankie twiddled her necklace. "Is there really any other flavor?"

Vandon topped her coffee off. "Just coffee for me. I have to get going in a few minutes."

"It's too bad you can't go with us today."

Vandon settled at the bar, nursing her coffee. "I would, but I've been taking our neighbor Mrs. Pinkerton to Breakwater ever since she broke her ankle. That's where she attends."

Raines entered the room looking like he'd stuck his finger in a light socket. "Morning, ladies."

Chapter 8

Frankie pulled into the Fort Hill church of Christ parking lot and looked at her passengers. "Ready?"

Melody grabbed her purse. "Yes, but I can't believe you made us late. I hate being late."

"Come on, babe. We can't change it now." Raines held the door open for Melody.

They slipped into the building as a man who looked like a male model stood behind the pulpit. Frankie sighed, thankful the back row had several spots for her to sit.

She slid into the pew, directly behind a couple sitting with four teenage girls. One of the girls reeled around and gave Frankie a dirty look. Frankie pulled her brows together and stared back at the girl, fighting the urge to stick her tongue out at her.

The girl's mother put her arm around her and whispered something in her ear before landing apologetic eyes on Frankie. Frankie bestowed a half smile on the woman before moving her attention to the preacher.

Melody elbowed Frankie and followed her line of sight. Trying her best to whisper, "I wonder if the preacher's single. He's gorgeous."

Raines gave Melody the stink eye, and she grinned. Frankie just shook her head. That would be a hard no. It wouldn't matter if he were the best-looking man alive.

The preacher's voice boomed across the auditorium. "We need those who will stand for the truth, who refuse to turn to the right or left. Those with tender hearts who are willing to repent when they have sinned. We need those who know and follow God's law."

The screen came to life behind the preacher, displaying a picture of a Bible. "Dear people, could it be that we need to wipe the dust from our Bibles?"

Frankie glanced at her watch—less than an hour to go.

A brief trickle of shame punctured her heart, but she quickly pushed it away.

"In Hosea, Chapter 4, verse 6, God said His people are destroyed because of a lack of knowledge. Are we those people even today?"

He glanced across the auditorium. "Let's make this personal. Ask yourself if you take time to study the Bible. Do you? Do you refuse to share it with others? Or do you speak up in love when opportunities arise?

"Many study their Bibles to try and prove some-one wrong. Is this you? Or do you peruse the pages with an open and honest heart? Do you set aside time to study the Word?"

"It's sad when we live in a country trying to push God out of its culture, eliminate Him from our schools, erase Him from the public mindset, and make fun of Him on national television. It's sad when we mock Him in His churches by not demand-ing truth, standing for the truth, and speaking out against error."

A throbbing sensation assaulted Frankie's temple, and she closed her eyes. She couldn't deal with a headache on top of everything else. She grabbed a couple of painkillers from her purse and headed to the water fountain.

After choking down the pills, she headed to the auditorium, almost colliding with Alex Foster as he came out of the men's bathroom. Her heart went haywire, and even with shaking legs, she managed to push past him and return to her seat.

Her fingers coiled into tight balls as she stared at the PowerPoint with unseeing eyes. How had she forgotten Alex Foster attended this church when they were younger?

Would she ever be rid of him?

Chapter 9

Frankie slipped her flip-flops off and stepped off the boardwalk. Her toes seemed to melt into the warm sand. Despite the near-perfect day, only a few people scattered on the beach.

Behind her, Melody gasped. She poured white sand from her shoes and wiggled her toes. "Oh, wow, this feels good and so warm."

Frankie's eyes sparkled as her lips twitched into a grin. Raines lumbered down the boardwalk, loaded with their canopy and chairs.

She and Melody each grabbed a chair. "I don't know how Melody puts up with your stubborn self. We told you we could carry our chairs."

A mischievous grin slid across his face. "She wouldn't know what to do without me."

Melody cocked her head like she was considering her response. Instead of disagreeing, she nodded. "It's crazy how soft and white this sand is."

They sat under the canopy's shade a few minutes later, spraying sunscreen on. Melody scanned the area, a soft smile playing across her face. "Tell me again why you didn't want to move here."

Frankie paused with the sunscreen in midair. "My friends live in Arkansas."

Raines pitched his Samsung device into a plastic container in Melody's bag. "It's less than two hours by plane and a few more driving."

Melody cut her eyes at Raines, scolding him without saying a word. "We will miss you, though. It's not like I want you to move, but your daddy did."

Frankie threw a chip on the ground, and a seagull grabbed it within seconds. A second one landed and looked at Frankie like it expected her to throw it a chip. "I know that."

Melody threw a chip on the ground close to the other seagull. The other one ran over and tried to take it away. When he couldn't win the chip, he stared back and forth from Frankie to Melody.

She threw a few more chips in between the seagulls with a giggle. "My parents always took us to the beach on the East Coast. I mean, it's beautiful, but this is like, wow. So maybe you'll end up loving it here."

Raines took a swig of water and headed toward the waves. He paused and grinned at Frankie. "The flags are green, so it's good to go."

"That's right. Safety first, always." Frankie rested her eyes on Melody, looking for the words to explain herself. "You know how much I've always loved traveling around Arkansas?"

Melody's gaze followed Raines as he waded along the shore. "I know it. I remember the first time your daddy took the youth group hiking."

The sun peeked out from behind the white cloud and landed on them. Frankie pulled her ballcap low. "That trip is where I first discovered my love for waterfalls."

"Yep. You were enthralled." Melody grinned. "And there for a minute, we didn't think Larry would make it to the waterfall."

"Yes! Raines had to help him. But after that, he went on a health kick. He was determined to lose that extra weight."

"Oh, yes."

"That's also when you and Raines started talking." Frankie made a kissy face.

Melody crinkled her nose and waved a hand at Frankie. "You used to drive me crazy making those silly kissy faces when we were younger."

The drone of a jet flying overhead drowned Frankie out. After it passed, she cocked her head. "Well, you kept denying your feelings."

She popped a chip in her mouth and shrugged. "We were so different and too young to date. Not to mention, I was a tomboy and had no intention of ever dating anyone."

Frankie nodded. "I remember. You ran from boys while I chased them." Her mind drifted to Alex Foster. She had been such a silly girl.

Melody's eyes widened. "I still can't believe you tased Alex Foster."

After a few inward cringes and pangs of regret, Frankie shrugged. "Not my finest moment."

Melody leaned halfway out of her chair, her face glowing with mischievousness. "Was that worse than your first kiss?"

After that look, Frankie should've known that whatever Melody had to say would be ridiculous. "That was not my first kiss."

"You kissed someone before Alex? Do tell." The ridiculousness continued. Maybe Melody enjoyed watching Frankie squirm.

It was Frankie's turn to widen her eyes. Widen? More like bugging them out so hard they could've landed in the sand. "What? No. No, I most certainly did not."

"Then it was your first kiss." Melody flipped her palms up and landed a satisfied smirk on Frankie. "And maybe you can get a repeat since y'all are partners."

Frankie gasped as a ribbon of excitement coursed through her belly. She had news for Melody – that would never happen. Not in a million years. No matter what her belly did.

"Believe me, Alex Foster was not a willing or active participant in that kiss." She squinted her eyes at Melody for good measure. "Not that it matters. He probably hates me, so there will certainly not be a second kiss."

Raines chose that moment to get out of the water. He passed Frankie and Melody by and greeted someone else. "Hey man, aren't you Frankie's neighbor?"

Frankie's head spun around, a pool of dread lining her ribcage. Sure enough, Alex Foster stood there shaking hands with Raines.

Looking right at Frankie.

Chapter 10

Frankie cast a glower at Alex before high-tailing it into the water. How would she ever live this one down? If he'd forgotten about that long-ago kiss, if he'd heard what she just said, he sure remembered now.

Humiliation burned her neck worse than it had ten years ago. She splashed water all over, doing her best to let it go. She didn't have much time before Melody went home, and she'd not let anything ruin this day.

Melody followed Frankie, entering the water like a bulldozer taking down an abandoned building. "Where do all the crabs come from?" Her voice tinged with the same fear she used to have over spiders. "I don't like them."

"From the holes." Frankie's jaw tightened as she scanned the beach. Raines and Alex had both disappeared. A weight lifted from her chest as she closed her eyes, breathing in the fresh air.

After adjusting her sunglasses, Melody lowered her head closer to the water. "I guess that was a stupid question."

A motorcycle rumbled in the distance as it headed out of the parking lot. The engine gunned as the driver headed toward Navarre.

"Not at all. They won't hurt you, though."

Frankie swished her hands through the crystal-clear water, searching for shells. A shell that looked to be almost as large as her hand disappeared under the sand. She dove into the water but couldn't grab it. Figures.

Melody shrieked as a near-translucent fish touched her leg. "What in the world was that?"

Frankie favored Melody with a grin. "A fish." She tried to talk in the most country twang possible. "Ain't you from Arkansas? You shouldn't let a tiny fish scare you."

She blew her cheeks out and chuckled. "Yep. I sure am from Arkansas, and I'm proud of it." Her eyes seemed to probe the water. "But I'm still getting out of this water until the fish are gone."

"Then you better stay gone 'cause they live here!"

Melody looked at Frankie straight-faced before she fought the waves out of the water.

Frankie let out a cackle until a massive wave knocked her down. She came up, spitting out water that left a taste of salt behind. As soon as she reached the shore, she plopped on her back.

Melody giggled and leaned close to Frankie's ear. "That serves you right."

Frankie made a face before heading back into the water close to where the shell had been. A kid that couldn't be more than ten or eleven floated by on a Pelican-shaped raft. Frankie checked the shore for his parents. The only person old enough to be his guardian had her phone up, taking self-ies.

"Hey, your kid doesn't need to go out so far." Just call Frankie Miss Busybody. Someone needed to be, though.

He'd gotten too close to deep water for Frankie's comfort. The flag had changed from green to yellow, so the water was more active. She started to yell at the girl again, but a fin poked out of the water before she got a word out.

And it was right by the kid.

Despite the sun beating down, Frankie's blood froze. Someone yelled her name. Someone else yelled for people to get out of the water. Instead of getting out, Frankie dove in, heading straight for the kid.

Another swimmer had the same idea. By the time they reached the kid, the shark had moseyed on. She grabbed ahold of the raft at the same time as the other swimmer grabbed the other side.

When they made it to shallow water, Frankie moved the raft. A wide smile parted her lips and landed on Alex Foster. She paused. "Thanks for the help."

A flicker of a smile broke through his lips. "That was awfully brave of you."

She bit her lower lip as a tickle spread through her stomach. "Thanks." Could she not say anything else? "But this doesn't change anything. We can't be partners."

One of his eyebrows slanted. "The thing is, we already are." He waded out of the water and grabbed a bag before walking down the boardwalk.

The boy's guardian turned out to be his sister, who promised through tears that she would never again allow her brother in the water without paying close attention. Raines went all medical on her and explained what could've happened.

The situation with the shark had ended better than it could have. If only the situation with Alex could.

Chapter 11

Less than six months. That's how long Frankie had to transform the cabins into a Christmas wonderland. If only she had an inkling of where to start. She'd be happy never to see another Christmas tree again. Not to mention the lights and music.

Again, she had to ask why Daddy would do this to her. She didn't want to deal with this. Especially Alex Foster. Daddy had never been controlling other than making her go to church. So why was he after death? She punched her pillow before flopping over and burying her head in the feathery softness. She sat on the side of the bed and glanced out the window. The sun peeked on the horizon, casting a bit of pink and purple light to the gray sky. She slid the window open and scowled when a smoky breeze wafted inside her bedroom. Was something on fire?

After slipping on a sweatsuit and pair of flip-flops, she hightailed it down the stairs and out the front door. She followed the line of smoke as it flitted from the back of the house.

Alex stood beside a pile of rubble with a rake in his hand. With the way her luck had been going, she should've known he'd still be living there. Maybe she could convince him that life in Perdido Key would be better than being her neighbor.

Wait. Perhaps he was just visiting his parents. She bit her bottom lip as she inwardly argued whether she should make her presence known. Better to get the inevitable over with. He needed to know she wouldn't be putting up with outdoor fires so close to her grandparents' home. She stomped across the lawn, gearing up for a fight.

He lifted his hand, his lips quivering as he fought a smile. "Morning."

Frankie's heart dropped, and she clamped her mouth shut. Whatever she had planned to say left her mind. As far as that went, everything she'd ever learned also left her.

No, no, no. This wouldn't work. She covered her mouth, pretending to yawn long enough to gain her composure. "Morning. Why are you burning things so early?"

He shrugged, and his quivering lips broke into a full-fledged smile. "It's just a few pieces of wood from Izzy's old doghouse. It's been out here so long that the wood's started to rot."

She couldn't stop the smile that sprang to her face as memories of being chased by a black and white dog flitted through her mind. "Oh, I remember Izzy."

"Yeah, he was a good dog. Mom and Dad couldn't bring themselves to get rid of his house after he passed." Alex's eyes took on a faraway look, and Frankie stepped closer to where he stood. She raised her hand to offer comfort but let it drop. "Or maybe it was me who couldn't get rid of it."

She took a step back. Alex wouldn't want comfort from her. He'd made that abundantly clear the last time she saw him.

Still, the look on his face as he remembered good times with Izzy struck her heart. "I'm sorry he's gone."

Alex took a step toward Frankie and lightly leaned on the rake. "Thanks. He sure loved you. I remember him chasing you all over this yard."

"Yeah, he was something." She looked around and stepped away from where he stood. "Where are your parents?"

"They moved to Montana after Ashley lost her first baby."

Her gaze sprang to his. That was not the best news. "I'm sorry. I didn't know Ashley lost a baby."

His gaze probed hers, almost like he wanted to make sure she meant what she said. "Yeah. She went through such a hard time dealing with her grief. She quit going to church for a while, and Mama and Daddy decided they needed to be there for her."

She swallowed as her throat constricted. She hated to hear that about Ashley. "Is she doing better?"

He nodded, and a look of pure contentment crossed his face. "She is. After prayerful studies, Ashley realized she couldn't blame God for her pain or loss. Our Heavenly Father loves us and will be here for us through our hard times. The day she understood that happened to be the day she felt better."

Frankie squirmed. Why did he have to bring that up? She knew God loved her and would be there. Of course, she did. Now happened to be a bad time to think about that, though. Change of subject, please. "Why Montana?"

He swiped the rake on the ground, raking at nothing in particular. "I know, right? That's way too cold for me, but they moved for work."

"So, you keep their yard done up for them?" Please say yes. Please say yes.

A look of pride crossed his face. "I bought the house last year after Ashley got pregnant again. They planned to sell but offered it to me before they put it on the market."

He didn't say yes. Something like a needle pricked Frankie right in the heart. Thankfully it happened fast, or her knees would've surely buckled. Alex lived here. He was not visiting.

She whirled about and raised both hands and palms out. "Well, that's just...something. I need to get back home."

A sigh came from Alex. "Frankie? I was so sorry to hear about your dad."

"Thank you." She had to keep moving, or her legs would certainly buckle then and there.

He took a few steps in the same direction. "I would've been at the funeral but was in Montana."

Why was he following her? Their conversation was over. "That's fine. You had no obligation to come."

"Hey, can we talk about everything?" He caught up to her, stopping close enough for her to get a whiff of smoke mixed with a woodsy mint.

Her pulse quickened, and she picked up the pace. "Sure thing, if you're talking about selling."

A swing to his head gave the answer before he even spoke. "No, I'm not selling."

She threw her hands up. "You can take on my part too, then. I'll sign it over to you as soon as possible."

He cocked his head and drilled his gaze into Frankie's. "I'm not doing that either. Not in a million years. Not that I'm going to, but I'd rather sell. Is this what Larry would have wanted?"

"Well, let's put this conversation on hold then." She backed a few feet away before dashing out of his yard. Her emotions had her mind whirling. Why did she have such a strong desire to touch that man? Even though he obviously didn't share that desire, she couldn't tamp it down. As soon as she entered the house, she ran to the bathroom and splashed cold water on her face. This would never work. If she kept going around him, she'd end up making a fool of herself like she had ten years ago.

One of them had to go. And since he made it clear it wouldn't be her, it would have to be him.

Chapter 12

It was odd how life could change in the blink of an eye. Just a few short months ago, Frankie never would've believed she'd be in Pensacola, Florida, dealing with Daddy's death while handling a massive project she hated.

She kept going back to the same question in her mind. Why? Did Daddy have a specific reason behind this? He had to. There's no way he'd put something this major into play without one.

Melody's giggles drifted from the back of the cabin before Raines let out a yelp. Frankie shook her head. There was no telling what Melody had done. A yellow flash, also known as Melody, zipped past Frankie with Raines on her tail. He snatched her by the shirt, and they both landed on the dirty carpet.

Raines had a blue paint streak on his arm and down the side of his white shirt. Frankie couldn't stop herself from giggling along with Melody.

Melody eyed Raines as he stepped into the washroom. She grasped Frankie's wrist as a big grin etched across her face. "I haven't heard you laugh like that in quite some time. I missed it."

Frankie looked down a second before meeting Melody's teary-eyed gaze. "I missed it, too. I'm almost ready to stop allowing grief to run my life."

"I wish we could stay longer than a week, but you know...jobs get in the way of unlimited time off."

Frankie snorted. "I should be working at The Lily Pad, getting ready to marry the man of my dreams. Instead..." She didn't finish the sentence.

A tan Ford Ranger stopped in front of the cabin, interrupting Frankie's line of thought. Happy to have an excuse to leave Raines to deal with his playful wife, Frankie excused herself to meet the contractor.

After greeting Clarence Little, they made their way to the first guest cabin. Frankie stepped inside and gasped.

A small kitchenette and a white table with four matching chairs lined the left side of the room, while a seating area with a loveseat and sofa flanked the fireplace. The first bedroom had a queen-sized bed, side table, and small dresser, while the second had two bunk beds. The only bathroom had white subway tile lining the walls, a shower, and a newer-looking toilet and sink.

Clarence cocked his head. "This has been well done. I thought you said the cabins were all a mess."

Frankie bit her bottom lip as she swiveled around. "Daddy said the cabins would need to be remodeled. Let's see what the rest of them look like." She stepped through the door and met Alex Foster's raised brow.

Great.

He motioned toward the cabin, a sly grin curling his lips upward. "What do you think?"

Her eyes lingered on his lips, and for a moment, she thought of the way they had felt against hers that day more than ten years ago. She jolted herself back to reality—no reason to think of that since it would never happen again.

Casting a glance behind her, she nodded, doing her best to shake off the unsettled feeling in her stomach. "An unexpected...surprise."

Clarence stuck a beefy hand out to Alex. "Hello, I'm Clarence Little. Which company did you hire to do the work?"

Alex tugged at his collar as a flush crept up his neck. "My buddies from church helped me with the first three cabins." He gazed down the gravel and dirt road. "We haven't started on the rest yet."

He nodded his approval. "Who are your buddies? I may need to hire 'em."

"Alvin Griffin, Gareth Davenport, and his twin brother, Cody."

"I'll admit I'm impressed. You fellas do good work."

"Appreciate that." A smile the size of the cabin door graced Alex's face. "Tell me, where do you attend church?"

It was Clarence's turn to redden. "Well, I can't say I'm going anywhere right now."

Alex clapped Clarence on the back as they made their way down the road. "I'd like to invite you to Fort Hill church this Sunday. It would be an honor to have you visit."

Clarence eyed Alex for a few seconds like he was sizing him up before nodding. "All right. You got yourself a deal."

A grin split Alex's face, and he beamed. "Come on, Frankie. Let's go check out the rest of the cabins."

Before they got too far, Frankie's phone rang. Anxious to see if Simon had made any headway on getting Alex to sell out, she jumped. "Hello."

"Frankie?" a female voice echoed from the other end of the line.

"Yes, this is Frankie."

"Hey, girl, this is Keatyn Davenport, I used to be a Griffin. You may not remember me, but Mama taught you in Sunday school during the summer. Cordelia gave me your number."

"I sure do remember you. How are you?"

"So great. I missed getting to talk to you at church Sunday."

"Yeah, sorry about that."

"We're having a cookout tonight and would love for you to come and bring your friends."

A no almost came out, but Frankie paused. She could talk to the preacher, and Keatyn could help get Alex to sell.

"Okay, what time?"

"Six - I'm texting the details now."

"Great. See you then. Thanks for the invite, Keatyn."

Alex stopped in his tracks and met Frankie's gaze. "You must be going to Keatyn's cookout."

"Yes, why?" Dread mixed with something else close to attraction crept up her spine.

"No reason." One shoulder bobbed up, and he grinned. "I'll be there. Want to ride together?"

Absolutely not.

She'd rather walk.

"That's okay. I'll be dropping Melody and Raines off at the airport on the way."

He waved a hand as if he understood, but Frankie could've sworn he looked disappointed before he walked away.

Chapter 13

S izzling grilled shrimp full of Louisiana spices wafted through the air. Alex's mouth watered as he waited for Gareth to finish grilling. Frankie claimed a lounge chair off to the side of the patio and took a sip of whatever she'd gotten to drink.

In the ten or so years since Alex had seen her, he'd thought about her in passing from time to time. Mostly, he thought of her during her many times of loss. He'd been in Japan when her mother passed, so he'd missed being there to support her family. He'd attended both her grandparents' funerals. Oddly, he couldn't remember seeing her at either of them. He figured she'd been hiding in plain sight. She was still in high school, so he doubted he would've noticed her then. But now? Now he couldn't miss her. Who could miss a woman with eyes like that? He shook his head, doing his best to kill that line of thinking. She had convinced herself she no longer liked him. She thought whatever childhood crush she had on him all those years ago was gone. She'd attempted to make her misguided feelings clear on more than one occasion since she'd moved next door.

At Keatyn's request, he shuffled toward where the object of his thoughts sat alone. "Hey." Why did he feel like Keatyn had ulterior motives?

"Hey." She looked away.

He stuffed his hands in the pockets of his shorts. "So, how do you like being back?"

The space between her eyebrows crinkled, and she shrugged. Whatever she looked at must be enthralling.

His gaze flickered in the direction that had captured her attention. Nothing enthralling. She wasn't even looking toward the Gulf – just the driveway. "Cat got your tongue?" Well, that sounded ridiculous.

The corners of her lips twitched, and she met his gaze. "You have the greenest eyes I've ever seen. There was a guy with hair as red as yours on a Halloween movie I watched one time, but his eyes weren't as green as yours."

"That's cool. I think."

A full-fledged grin appeared, and she seemed to be at ease for once. "That was probably weird and random, but I've wanted to tell you that ever since I saw the movie."

"Not weird or random. It's cool that you thought of me." Now, it was his turn to break eye contact.

He knew it! She'd been thinking of him even before they reconnected.

"Well, I thought of the hair color. You know, because it's so red." She stuck her hands underneath her legs and swallowed.

"Did your friends make it home safely?"

"Yep." Her lips pressed together, and she nodded one large nod. "They're already back in Arkansas."

"Glad to hear it." Why did he feel like this? He closed his eyes and took a breath. "Can we talk about our situation with the cabins?"

Her neck snapped in his direction. "I'm glad you brought it up." Her body seemed to stiffen. "Will you please sell your part to me?"

The driveway suddenly became more appealing to look at. "I'm not interested in selling."

She gripped the arm of the lounge chair. Her voice raised an octave when she spoke. "Why not?"

Gareth glanced in their direction with a raised brow. Alex tried to speak in a low tone so she would get the hint. "Because."

"Well, I'm not interested in being your partner." Her earlier carefree expression disappeared, replaced by a stony face.

"That's too bad." His jaw ticked. If only she'd put as much energy into getting the cabins ready as she did in getting him to sell. "Please don't ask me to sell to you again. The answer will always be no. Besides, I think you and I both know better than that."

Frankie stood and brushed past Alex. She stopped when she reached Keatyn. After speaking with her for a minute or so, she walked away.

Without even saying goodbye.

Chapter 14

Frankie pulled into an empty parking spot at the Pensacola Children's Home and traded a glance with Vandon. "This place is massive. We could totally use this area for the Christmas festivities."

Vandon pushed the car door open. She paused, glancing at Frankie. "Now, how fun would that be for the kids who are already here every day?"

"I guess you're right." As Frankie walked up the path, she couldn't escape the thoughts of touring the place with Daddy. She searched the area until her eyes landed on the house he'd had lived in before the adoption. She remembered how proud he had been to show her around the day they visited around five years ago.

Vandon opened the door and tapped her foot. "Come on, slowpoke."

After taking another look at the house, she followed Vandon inside. "How long do we have before the tours start?"

"Oh, about thirty minutes. We'll tour two or three homes, then break for lunch and the speaker before finishing the rest."

By the time lunch rolled around, Vandon's hands were shaking. A slight frown tugged at Frankie's lips as they waited in line to make their plates. "Are you okay?"

"I don't know. My heart's beating so fast." She stared into space for a few seconds before a light seemed to go off. "I need to eat."

One of the house parents appeared beside Vandon with a piece of strawberry candy. "Here, take this until you can get your plate made."

Frankie scurried to a table and piled a plate full of fried shrimp and all the fixings. Vandon wasted no time digging in.

A few hours later, Vandon had her sugar under control, and they'd toured almost all the houses. Next up, they'd get to go to Daddy's old place. Frankie licked her lips and rubbed her palms down her khaki shorts. Daddy lived here as a kid. This is where he met Mama after she moved here. Mama's parents had drowned in a boating accident when Mama was a child, so both Frankie's Mama and Daddy had lived here for a short time. Luckily for Mama, her grandma's sister took her in. Luckily for Daddy, he and Mama went to the same school in

Pensacola after he was adopted. The stars aligned in their favor, that was for sure.

A blur of blonde hair pushed past Frankie and Vandon as they walked through the door of Daddy's old house. The blur turned out to be a girl who looked to be sixteen or so. Frankie knew her from somewhere.

She paused on the front steps and narrowed her brown eyes at Frankie. "Excuse *you*."

Frankie's mouth fell open. "Excuse me? You're the one who ran into me."

The girl marched back up the steps, stopping an inch from Frankie's face. "You rich people have nothing better to do than come in here staring at the poor little kids with nowhere to go. You have no business here, so yes, you."

A woman Frankie instantly recognized as the woman from church made her way to where Frankie and the rude girl stood. "I'm so sorry. I'm Lunelle Baldridge, the house mother. Rhnae, please apologize to our guest."

That's where she knew the girl from. She'd been the one who gave Frankie a dirty look last Sunday.

Rhnae chortled as she curtsied. "Dear lady, please accept my humble apologies for telling you the truth."

Frankie swallowed the laugh that tickled her tongue. Lunelle obviously didn't think it was funny since she pointed toward another room. Vandon gasped, so she must not think it was funny either.

Frankie stuck her hand out. "I'm Frankie Kingston. Nice to meet you."

"Frankie Kingston?" Rhnae stopped in her tracks, staring at Frankie. "The one doing the Christmas camp?"

"That's right. My daddy lived here in this exact home when he was a kid."

"Seriously?" Rhnae's face softened a smidge.

"Yes, seriously." Frankie couldn't say why, but having the girl look at her with a bit of acceptance instead of disdain felt nice.

Lunelle put her hand on her hip. "I told you to go to your room."

"I'm sorry, I just got so excited when I heard Christmas camp." She headed down the hallway and paused with her hand on the doorknob. "I really am sorry for being rude."

Frankie offered a smile. Who knows how Frankie would act if she were living here? Weren't they both orphans, in a way? "Apology accepted."

Rhnae's lips curved as she disappeared into the room.

Frankie held her breath, trying to decide if she was about to make a mistake. No matter, it's what Daddy would do. "Would it be possible for Rhnae to volunteer at the camp? Maybe she could help paint or decorate."

Lunelle tapped her chin, her gaze lingering on the door Rhnae had disappeared behind. "I'll check into it and call you later this week. Will that work?"

Even though Frankie said yes, she prayed her spontaneous gesture wouldn't turn out to be a disaster.

Chapter 15

Frankie slid into the pew behind the Baldridge family as the song leader stepped away from the pulpit. Rhnae swiveled in her seat and smiled, displaying deep dimples. Frankie found herself smiling back as the preacher, Gareth Davenport, took the song leader's place.

He wasted no time diving into his sermon. "If you have your Bibles, turn with me to the first chapter of Colossians. The first four chapters contain a beautiful letter showing us how Christ should be at the heart and core of the Christian life."

As he read the verses, Frankie got lost, flipping through the pages of her Bible. By the time she found Colossians, he'd finished reading it. She gave up and pulled up her phone's Bible app.

Gareth continued, "It's important for us to grasp the concept that if we are in Christ and Christ is in us, then we have access to every spiritual blessing that God intends for His people today. Turn with me to verse 3 of Ephesians chapter 1."

Even though the screen behind Gareth displayed the verse, she followed along on her app. "Let us read it together. Blessed be the God and Father of our Lord Jesus Christ, who has blessed us with every spiritual blessing in the heavenly places in Christ."

"Paul tells us in Colossians chapter 2, verse 10 we are complete in Him, who is the head of all principality and power. Let me suggest to you that those who say they're a Christian, yet they are always unhappy or constantly complaining, well, I can promise you that person is probably not living a Christ-centered life. In fact, they are probably like Jonah, and they're running away from God. A Christ-centered Christian will realize what wonderful blessing they have in Christ, and they're not going to allow day-to-day disappointments to keep them down."

"Remember how Paul said he can do all things through Christ who strengthens him? He relied on Christ no matter what he was dealing with. But sadly, some lean on their own wisdom and knowledge for spiritual life. But human wisdom is vain and deceptive and will leave you spiritually bankrupt."

Gareth's voice rose an octave as he continued his sermon. "Let's go to Proverbs chapter 14, verse 12. There is a way that seems right to a man, but its end is the way of death."

Frankie shifted in the seat and allowed her mind to wander. Daddy had always told her to run *to*

Christ and never away. He kept a good attitude toward Christ even after being told he was dying of cancer. He'd studied the Bible with Frankie up until his last days.

Why didn't she have the same attitude? Could it be her life centered around something other than Christ? She cocked her head, staring at the preacher but not seeing or hearing anything. Memories of Mama and Daddy skipped through her mind. Days of love and laughter had filled her childhood.

A longing filled her heart as she remembered Mama kissing her good night while she waited on Daddy to read her a bedtime story. They both had such good hearts. They loved God. What had happened to Frankie's heart?

The song leader led the congregation in a closing hymn, snapping Frankie's mind back to the present. Thank goodness. She didn't need to allow her mind to dwell on such things.

She left the church before the last song ended. It was better that way.

Later that night, Frankie curled up in a hammock in her backyard. Figuring a little music would help her heart and soul, she played Daddy's favorite old-school rock album by Bon Jovi.

"I'll be there for you!" she sang along to the beautiful words she'd grown to love over the years.

"Frankie?"

Her heart leaped out of her chest as she rose out of the hammock. Alex. Again. She turned the music down, and her lips flattened. "Alex."

He scratched the back of his neck. "I heard the loud music and wanted to make sure you're all right."

"Of course, I'm all right." She pushed a few curls out of her face. It was no use. Flyaway curls couldn't be stopped. "Can't a girl sing along to Bon Jovi?"

He had enough sense to look embarrassed. "Well, yeah. It's just so loud. I'm surprised Mrs. Pinkerton from down the road hasn't shown up at your front door. Just be thankful her ankle is not quite healed yet."

She clicked the off button before making her way to the back door. "Sorry if I bothered you. Have a good night, Alex."

His countenance dropped as he started to walk away. He paused and probed Frankie's gaze before opening the wooden gate to his yard.

Why did he look like he lost a puppy? Probably trying to soften her up so she would give up on the idea of him selling. He used to talk her into sharing her favorite candy bars with him by giving her that sad face. Too bad for him. She just so happened to be immune to his fake charms. She'd been hurt enough, so it was best she protect her heart.

She went straight to her bedroom and pulled up the internet. She blinked a few times as she tried to decide what to search for to get him to sell the cabins to her. Her fingers got busy typing as soon as it hit her.

How to get a neighbor to move.

Chapter 16

Alex pulled his John Deere mower onto the trailer and wiped the sweat off his brow. A group of kids and house parents waved as they walked down across the freshly mowed lawn. He waved back as he grabbed the weed eater before closing the trailer gate.

He found himself searching for Bon Jovi on his music app. For some reason, he had the urge to listen to some rock music.

The reason why hit him as soon as the music played over his earbuds.

Dark curly hair and hazel eyes drifted across his mind, and he balked. That little girl who used to follow him around had turned out to be a breathtaking woman.

Just his luck.

It would've been easier if she'd grown up to be less attractive. Especially since she went out of her way to let him know she held zero interest in him. He couldn't figure out who she wanted to convince more. Him or herself.

She wanted him to think she couldn't stand to be in the same room as him. What he didn't understand was why. Maybe it was time to pay her a visit to get to the bottom of her actions.

That's what he would do. Soon.

But in the meantime, he needed a distraction. Hadn't he seen a flyer asking for volunteers to clean the beaches to help with sea turtle nesting? That would be a worthwhile cause.

A skinny woman shot out the front door of the main office and ran to a beat-up maroon Ford Explorer. She fell into the door, holding her side, sobbing.

Alex swallowed and scanned the area for a woman to console her. No such luck. Normally, he wasn't one to insert himself in someone's business, but could he just walk away and call himself a Christian?

He leaned the weed eater on the side of the trailer and walked toward the woman. "Ma'am?"

The woman jerked around, wiping a long blonde strand of hair away from her face. She reminded him a tiny bit of his mother. "I'm sorry." Her voice cracked as she bent her steps toward the car.

"Do you need some help?" Alex stopped a couple of feet away from the car.

She met his gaze but lowered her eyes before she spoke. "No one can help me."

He looked around, hoping someone would magically appear to help him figure out what to say in this situation. "I'll certainly try." He tried to smile in such a way that she would be at ease. "I'm Alex, by the way."

Hopeful eyes landed on Alex, seeming to see him for the first time. "My name is Lottie. I'm a drug addict here to see my sixteen-year-old daughter who was taken away because of my own stupidity." She swallowed. "Recovering drug addict."

He glanced toward the office. "Would they not let you see her?"

She made a choking sound and wiped her eyes. "Not them."

Oh.

Lottie blew her nose and continued, "It was her. She refused to see me."

Now would be a good time for someone to appear who was good at consoling people. But since no one did, it was up to Alex.

"I don't know the story, so it's hard for me to give advice. I will say it looks like you're trying to rebuild your relationship with your daughter, and I think that's a great step toward healing."

"You some kind of preacher or something?"

"Me? Oh, no, I'm a landscaper. But more importantly, I'm a Christian."

"Thanks for listening." She pulled at the door handle on the Explorer. "I better get going. I've embarrassed my daughter enough."

"Do you live in town?"

"I'm staying at...a hotel until I can find a job and a place I can afford." She looked at her feet.

"Do you go to church anywhere?"

"Nope."

He pulled a card out of his pocket and tried to hand it to her. "I'd be honored if you'd be my guest at the Fort Hill church of Christ this Sunday."

She blinked a few times like she was stunned, keeping her hands at her side. "Did you hear me say I'm a drug addict?"

He cocked his head and attempted to hand her the card again. "I heard you say you're a recovering drug addict. Either way, you're welcome in the Lord's church."

Chapter 17

Frankie walked around the cabin. If she didn't get busy with the remodel, she'd never be able to hold a Christmas festival this year.

Maybe she should use some of her savings to hire someone to help. That's probably the best idea she'd had in a long time.

Happy she'd come up with a good plan, she skipped outside to find Vandon. She couldn't help but smile at how Vandon sat around the fire pit talking to an orange and white cat.

The cat looked at Vandon like it understood, so who was Frankie to question their conversation?

A giggle escaped Frankie as she walked up to the pair. "The cat seems to be a good listener."

"Better than my late husband, that's for sure." The cat jumped onto Vandon's lap, and she ran her hand down its head.

"You were married?"

"Spent forty years of my life married to my Carl." Vandon's face lit up with the mention of her late husband. "I lost him last year, and that's when Larry asked me to move into his parent's home. Said he wanted me to take care of it, but I know he just wanted to take care of me."

Frankie claimed an empty chair and propped her elbow on the arm. "Daddy knew your husband too?"

Vandon's hand froze on the cat's back. "Don't you know who I am, Frankie?" The cat swiveled its head and tried to nip Vandon's hand. She started rubbing again, and it settled down, seemingly content.

Frankie couldn't put her finger on the reason, but a tremor crossed her spine. "I guess I don't."

"Carl and I were your dear daddy's house parents at the children's home." She stopped petting the cat again. "I'm sorry for not telling you before now. I thought you knew."

Vandon's presence at the house now made sense. Daddy would've wanted to take care of his house mother.

Frankie laid her hand on Vandon's shoulder. "I'm so glad you told me. It's me who should be sorry for forgetting you. I remember now that we met once before when I was a kid."

"Don't you worry about that." Vandon grasped Frankie's hand in her own. "I'm convinced your daddy wanted us to be here for one another. See, he knew I had no one after Carl passed, and I know he didn't want you to be alone."

Frankie's heart thudded as it hit her. Vandon was right. Daddy wanted her to have Vandon, and Vandon to have her.

She'd been looking at things all wrong. She wasn't alone after all. Daddy had made sure of that.

Later that afternoon, Frankie and Vandon pulled into the Walmart parking lot. Vandon put her hand on the door handle. "Don't forget to pick me up in an hour."

"I won't forget. I'm just going across the street."

Vandon grabbed her purse and looked at Frankie. "Okay, then I'll see you in one hour."

A whiff of disinfectant spray overwhelmed Frankie as soon as she entered the local video store. She really needed to pick up a few outdoor video cameras, or the strong disinfectant smell would force her to leave. That had always been her least favorite odor. She'd rather smell a skunk.

She pretended to rub her nose as she glanced around the store. The only other customer, a woman with a camera in her hands, stood at the counter.

A man who reminded Frankie of Barney Fife came out of the back of the store and handed the woman a box. He glanced at Frankie. "I'll be with you in a few minutes."

"No rush. I'm just looking around for now."

They had a wide variety of video cameras. She needed at least four of them if her plan to get Alex to think she was a crazy neighbor was going to work. Pointing a bunch of cameras at the neighbor's house had been among the first suggestions the internet provided.

When the other customer left, the man walked up to Frankie. "What can I help you find?"

"I need four wireless outside cameras. What are the most reasonably priced options?"

He grinned and motioned for her to follow him. "It just so happens we have a four-pack of the ones I use at my own home right here." He pulled the box out. "And the best part is they won't break the bank."

After paying for the cameras, she glanced at her watch. She had three hours left before her flight to Arkansas. That should be plenty of time to install the cameras.

Let Operation Make Alex Sell commence.

Chapter 18

Fritters of nerves balled up in the pit of Frankie's stomach. If she had a choice, she'd never go to another funeral.

Yet here she sat at the Hazen Funeral Home. Saying goodbye to one of her favorite school librarians.

Alone.

Again.

Melody and Raines were on a cruise to Mexico, celebrating their anniversary. So that left Frankie showing her support without them. Mrs. Beverly had been too good to Frankie for her to stay away. No matter how uncomfortable she was.

Soft lighting played into the creamy brown walls. Amazing Grace drifted from the speakers in the ceiling. Closing her eyes, she worked to do nothing but listen to the song.

The librarian from the Hazen Public Library, Eloise Jenner, smeared lip balm on and glanced at Frankie.

"She never failed to visit me at the library every single week."

The woman sitting beside Eloise gave a partial smile. "She volunteered to help me with school events. I don't know what I'll do without her. I'm Jackie Briggs, one of the second-grade teachers."

After exchanging greetings, a brittle smile dashed across Frankie's face. Mrs. Beverly had been a source of comfort for Frankie after Mama's death. It was comforting to hear stories about her.

Raking her dry tongue over her lips, Frankie settled into the seat when everyone got quiet. She'd be stopping by the tea shop later, that's for sure.

The Funeral Director stepped up to the podium, a sad yet understanding expression on his face. "Good morning, friends and family."

After the thoughtful and beautiful service honoring Mrs. Beverly's life, Frankie said her goodbyes and promised to stop by the library before leaving town.

She glided past several groups of people with a Pineapple Punch on her mind.

Before she reached her borrowed car, someone called her name. She swiveled around, immediately locking gazes with Brayden Parker.

"I was hoping I'd see you here." His arms circled her before she could so much as say a word.

The air in her lungs faded as he took a step back. For a second, it seemed like he was going to kiss her. Thankfully, he didn't. Even a kiss on the cheek would be way awkward. "Hi, Brayden."

He smiled at a few people as they passed by. He tugged his shoulder-length sandy blonde locks out of the ponytail holder. "I hate that it's under these circumstances, but I'm happy you're here."

"Oh?" She eyed Brayden. Happy she's here? Where did that come from?

"Do you have plans this morning?"

"I'm heading over to Cozy Corner to grab a drink." She paused. What would a little company hurt? "Wanna come?"

Brayden's old flame, Emily Martin, gave Brayden a dirty look as she walked past them. She stopped by a group of people congregating beside a Mercedes SUV.

A woman Frankie had never seen openly gawked at Frankie and Brayden. Frankie narrowed her eyes as she stared back.

What in the world? Things must not have ended well between the two of them.

Brayden followed Frankie's line of sight. He glared at the group and ran a hand through his hair. "Can I ride with you?"

An offer like this would've had her heart singing less than three months ago. But now? Not so much as a flutter. "Sure."

Cozy Corner Nutrition reminded Frankie of happier days with its super cool purple couch and colorful teal walls.

The only employee on duty flew around the counter when she noticed Frankie. "Oh my! I know it's only been a couple of months, but I've missed you coming in."

"I've missed stopping by. No one else can make my drinks just how I like them."

They hugged before the employee wagged her finger. "Don't you worry, I'll have you a Pineapple Punch whipped up in no time." Laughter hung in her gaze as she looked from Frankie to Brayden. "What'll you have today?"

He licked his lips and tapped his chin. "Lemme get a Peanut Butter Banana Shake."

"Coming right up."

Three girls that couldn't have been more than seventeen bounced inside. Giggles filled the room. Oh, to be so carefree again.

Frankie and Brayden claimed a table while they waited for their drinks.

Brayden looked around, and a cheeky smile split his lips. "We've spent many an hour here, haven't we?"

"Yep. We had the best group of friends ever."

The employee set their drinks down. "Enjoy!"

Frankie wasted no time slurping some of it down. The tart sweetness of pineapple tickled her tongue, and she took a moment to bask in the taste.

He sucked on his straw, his line of sight drifting out the window. "I should've asked you out before you moved."

Frankie didn't know what to say. Her breath hitched in her throat as she met his gaze.

His shoulder bobbed, and his mouth formed a straight line. "Yeah, I figured that would be a shock." He bit into his bottom lip. "Will you agree to go on a date with me? I think we can make a long-distance relationship work."

Frankie couldn't stop the bit of sadness from lining her smile. "I don't know how to answer that."

She should tell him no. That he waited too long time to ask her out. His wandering eyes had never landed on her. He'd dated at least three girls over the past year while keeping Frankie dangling as his friend. It wouldn't have been so hard if he hadn't flirted with her, giving her hope he was on the verge of asking her out.

He took Frankie's hand and rubbed his thumb across her fingers. "Just say yes."

This man had the looks that always made Frankie forget her name. He reminded Frankie of a rockstar from forty years ago. So, what made her hesitate to say yes? Her dream of dating Brayden could come true. Right here and now.

What was the holdup?

Red hair and green eyes clouded her vision. No way would she allow herself to have feelings for Alex. No, thank you.

Even though a slight frown belied her answer, she nodded at Brayden. "Yes."

Chapter 19

When Frankie drove into Des Arc, the first order of business was stopping by The Lily Pad. She pushed the dark brown door open and moseyed inside, propping her elbows on the counter.

"Can I get some service?" Her voice echoed throughout the building.

Jessica strolled in from the back room. When she laid eyes on Frankie, she stopped and pinned her arms across her chest. "I don't know that we serve the likes of you."

They each snorted laughs before hugging.

Frankie pulled back and pointed across the room. "Since when did we get new art supplies?"

Jessica followed Frankie's line of sight before waving her hand. "We ordered those before you left. Don't you remember?"

Frankie headed toward the kid's section, but a box of Fire Fishing Poles caught her attention. She stopped. "These are perfect."

"Perfect for what?"

"Roasting hot dogs and marshmallows at the camp." She pulled a pole out of the container. Surely that would be a good activity for the kids.

She twisted her lips and looked at Frankie like she'd said something ridiculous. "I thought you were doing a Christmas camp." Jessica picked a pole up and turned it over, scanning the back of the box.

"I'm no expert, but I bet we can have a bonfire even at Christmas." Frankie poked her tongue out.

After returning the pole, Jessica shrugged. "I guess you're right."

Frankie picked up a box of shortbread cookies and set them on the counter. She'd buy those for later. "I have a date with Brayden tonight."

Jessica froze. "Brayden?"

"Yep, and I don't want to go alone. Would you double with us?"

"Unless you have a magic wand or a man in your back pocket, I'll have to pass." She leaned close to Frankie like they were sharing a secret. "I'm single."

Frankie clicked her tongue. "I know that, silly. Brayden's cousin is in town."

A spark of interest crossed her features. "What cousin?"

"Max Coleman from Trumann."

Jessica's lips tugged downward. "I thought Brayden's cute cousin lived in DeValls Bluff."

"Yeah, but he moved to Trumann last year to take a job teaching at their high school."

"Ugh, I guess I'll come." She rang up the cookies before landing a sour face on Frankie. "Hopefully, he's not the ugly cousin."

A bark of laughter left Frankie as she paid for the cookies. "Me, too! Meet us at Dondie's at seven."

Just after seven, Frankie sat across from Brayden on the top floor of the restaurant. She'd always taken the place for granted when she lived in Des Arc. As she took inventory of their surroundings, she had a newfound appreciation.

Dondie's had always been the place to go for good fish and all the fixings. The location couldn't have been more perfect on the White River. The restaurant looked just like a two-story boat that you'd see floating down the river.

Brayden snickered, pulling her attention away from the decorations. The phone screen highlighted his features. That phone must have something interesting on it.

He'd asked her out only to stare at his phone. And to think she'd been waiting forever for this first date.

He finally peeled his eyes off the screen. "I'm sorry. Do you want me to put it down?"

"Nope." I mean, why would she? If he found what was on the phone more interesting than her, who was she to keep him from it?

Jessica lowered herself into the seat beside Frankie. "Sorry, I'm late."

Brayden laid the phone on the table. "No worries. But I'm sorry, Max isn't feeling well."

Her eyebrows raised, and she stood up. "Why didn't one of you call me?" She took a step away from the table, her face flushed.

Brayden raised himself out of his seat. "It's fine. We can all hang out tonight."

Even though Jessica shook her head, she took a tentative step toward the table. Her gaze darted to Frankie. "I don't want to hijack your first date. That wouldn't be right."

"It's fine." Frankie pulled the seat out. "Sit."

They spent the rest of the evening reminiscing about the good ole days, as Daddy always called them. Their date turned out much better than she thought.

Especially since Jessica stayed. They'd never been super close in school, but they'd not been enemies either. Even after working together the past year, they'd kept things friendly but hadn't become as close as they could have. Maybe this would be the beginning of a closer friendship.

She glanced around the table. If not for her and Jessica, then maybe for Brayden and Jessica.

Chapter 20

Alex grabbed his strawberry smoothie and wallet before heading out the door. His phone rang as he walked down the steps.

He glanced at the phone to see it was Mom calling. He had plenty of time before Bible class, but something told him not to answer.

He'd been texting with Ashley already this morning, so surely nothing was wrong. Still, he couldn't ignore a call from Mom.

"Good morning, Mom."

"Alex?"

"Yes'm. How are you?"

"I'm good. We all are great here. I just need a favor, son."

"Whatcha need?"

"My friend, Donna's daughter, will be coming to Pensacola next week. Will you show her around since she doesn't know anyone there?"

Alex stopped in his tracks. Why would Frankie have all those security cameras pointing at his house?

"Son?" Mom cleared her throat. "Are you there?"

He took another look at the cameras just as the front door opened. He waved at Miss Vandon before climbing into his truck.

"I'm still here. What were you saying?"

"You need to pay attention. I said I want you to spend some time with Sierra Wood next week."

"Who in the world is that?" He took inventory of the front porch and found it lacking. Maybe a few plants would make it look better.

"I told you, she's my friend Donna's daughter. She's starting a new job at Pensacola University and'll be there next week trying to find a home."

"What's that got to do with me?"

"She's a beautiful young woman, is what it has to do with you. And she'll be in a strange place all alone. I figured you'd be able to introduce her to some people and take her to church."

"Okay, Mom. I'll invite her to church."

"And out to eat?"

"I don't know about that, but church for sure. The ladies there will take care of her."

"I know they will. But I was hoping you'd take an interest in her."

"Mom."

"Son. You're pushing thirty years old and haven't shown a bit of interest in settling down."

He should've ignored the call after all.

"It'll happen sooner or later."

"Let's just hope it's sooner. Well, I need to get ready for service. I'll call you later with details about Sierra's arrival."

"Ok, love you."

"Love you, honey. Have a good day. Tell everyone at church I miss them."

His brow rose, and a smile touched his lips when he pulled into the church parking lot. The beat-up maroon Ford Explorer sat in one of the visitor parking spots.

By the time he made it to the front of the building, Lottie had been welcomed inside by a door greeter. She wrung her hands together as Alex walked inside the auditorium. She looked nervous as she slid into an empty pew. Scared even.

Alex stopped where she sat. "Do you mind if I sit with you, Miss Lottie?"

The relief on her face took Alex by surprise. What could have made her so nervous? Could this be the first time she'd ever gone to church?

After listening to a sermon about Boaz and Ruth, a girl marched up to Lottie. "What do you think you're doing here?"

Lottie's hand went to her throat. She paused, and eyes gutted with pain landed on Alex. "I was invited to come here."

The girl skewered Lottie with a fiery gaze. "Yeah, right."

Lunelle Baldridge from the Children's Home put her hand on the girl's arm. "Please don't be rude, Rhnae. Let's just go."

Understanding dawned on Alex. That must be Lottie's daughter.

What a coincidence that he invited Lottie to the same church her daughter goes to.

Coincidence? Maybe.

God's providence. Probably.

Chapter 21

Instead of listening to her inner voice, Frankie decided to ignore the anxiety. She missed Daddy so much that it hurt. How things would be different if he could be here.

He must've enjoyed the view from the cabin. It sure had no problem capturing Frankie's attention. She bet he spent time in this very spot by the window. How she longed to see him again.

A couple of squirrels frolicking in one of the trees grabbed her attention. How happy they seemed!

If only Frankie could gain a bit of that happiness.

An amused expression crossed her face. Surely, she wasn't jealous of squirrels.

She'd driven straight to the cabins from the airport, hoping to figure out the best route to fulfill Daddy's wishes. Not stare at squirrels in envy.

If Daddy were here, he'd have fake snow, hot cocoa, a bunch of Christmas booths, and a horse-drawn carriage. Santa Claus would probably even make an appearance.

But that's not Frankie.

She hated Christmas.

Well, hate may be too strong a word. Immensely disliked sounded better.

How would she ever turn this place into something that would live up to Daddy's standards?

The front door creaked open. Frankie spun around only to meet those blasted green eyes that seemed to haunt her.

A woman stepped inside behind him. An ache lurked behind Frankie's ribs. Maybe he had a girlfriend. Why hadn't she thought of that before? Why wouldn't he have a girlfriend? Any woman would be happy with that face.

Well, any woman except her. Ha. Liar. She would most certainly be happy with that face, but she'd never try to force herself on him.

Again, anyway.

"Good morning, Frankie." He nodded toward the woman who trailed behind him. "This is Lottie."

Frankie closed the space between them. She needed a better look at the woman. Wrinkles lined the woman's eyes and mouth, and her face seemed hollow. She had to be pushing fifty or even sixty, so she doubted Lottie was Alex's girlfriend.

"Hello, Lottie."

Lottie gaped at Frankie a good ten seconds before she spoke. "Nice to meet you."

Alex braced his arm on the countertop. "I was hoping Clarence would hire Lottie to help fix up the cabins."

"I haven't seen him so far this morning."

Even though her jaw twitched, Lottie's eyes never left Frankie. What was wrong with the woman?

Alex coughed. Maybe he was just as uncomfortable with Lottie as Frankie was. "Could you use some help?"

Yeah, she could use some help, but not from a drug addict. Frankie's eyes popped as she looked from Lottie to Alex. "I'm considering my options now." She sounded like a snob even to her own ears, but she had no desire to have a druggie around.

"Just so you know, I've been clean for six months." Lottie pulled a receipt out of her purse and scribbled something on it. "This is my number. Please call me if you decide to hire help. I promise if you give me a chance, you won't regret it."

Later that evening, Frankie watched Alex loading potted plants onto his front porch. One of the ways to get Alex to think she was unstable enough to buy her out had just landed in her lap. A gentle puff of laughter left Frankie as she headed to Alex's.

He looked at Frankie and wiped his brow. "What brings you over here?"

"I saw you with the plants and thought I'd save you from making a huge decorating mistake."

He scanned the area before placing a potted palm tree in the corner. "What do you mean? I figured you headed over to enjoy my company."

She screwed her face up, a look of disgust landing on her features. "That looks stupid there."

He stared at Frankie with his mouth hung open for a few seconds. He ignored her statement and put another plant beside the porch swing.

"You have no sense of style. That plant would look better over there." She pointed at the other end of the porch.

He pinched his lips together. "Did you come over here just to insult me?"

"Of course not." She moved one of the plants to the other side of the porch. "What's Lottie's story?"

He took a swig out of a water bottle before moving the plant back to the spot where he'd originally placed it. "Not mine to tell."

She shrugged. "I wasn't asking for gossip, Alex. I just didn't appreciate you putting me on the spot earlier."

His body froze. "Don't worry, I got your point. We both did. You don't want her working there."

She crossed her arms over her chest. "That's why I'm asking about her. What kind of job would she even qualify for?"

"Don't you need help painting and stuff since you decided to work on the main cabin by yourself?"

Her head jutted back. "What makes you say that?"

"Maybe the way you've shut me out ever since you got here?" He threw his hands in the air. "I don't know if you're doing it to spite me or yourself."

She rolled her eyes. Even though deep inside she knew he was right, she couldn't let him know that. "That's a bunch of bull."

He slowly shook his head, flipping his mouth into a line. "No, it is not. I mean, how many times have you asked me to sell?"

"Apparently not enough." Her lips narrowed as thin as paper. "Forget I said anything."

Chapter 22

Alex clicked the lock on his front door in place and tiptoed to his truck. Even though darkness covered the sky, the moon cast plenty of light to see where he was going.

He spent the next hour filling in holes and cleaning the beach so that the hatchling sea turtles would have a clear path to the water. If only people would pick up their trash and stop leaving holes in the sand, the sea turtles would have it so much easier.

As he left the beach, he pondered the day ahead. Or at least he tried to. He desperately wanted to get Frankie's dark curls and fiery eyes out of his mind. She wanted him to believe her feelings for him were in the past, but he knew better. He could see right through her act. Or maybe she'd convinced herself she had no feelings for him, and it would be up to him to help her see the truth.

A grin tugged at his lips as he thought of all the fun he could have, helping her realize she still had the same childhood crush on him.

When he closed his CPA business, he'd opted to use the same spot for Foster's Lawn Care. He had plenty of space for a building to house his equipment and keep the Homeowner's Association happy at home.

A ribbon of excitement tinged his tummy. The winning bid for the City of Pensacola lawn services had gone to him. This contract would put Foster's Lawn Care in a position he'd only dreamed of happening this quickly.

A text from Ashley dinged his phone. Mom wanted Ashley to remind Alex of his breakfast date with Sierra. He texted back, reminding Ashley and Mom it was not a date and he was leaving to meet her.

The Waffle House buzzed with customers as Alex climbed into a booth. Bacon and eggs sizzled on the grill, causing his stomach to growl. Sierra should be there any minute now.

A tall, attractive woman stepped inside. She smiled when she locked eyes with Alex and came straight to where he sat. "Alex?"

He hoisted himself to his feet, and a smile jotted across his lips. "Yes, ma'am. I assume you're Sierra."

Her silvery blonde locks flowed straight as a board to her chin. She tucked a few pieces behind her ear, reminding Alex of a shampoo commercial. "Thank you for meeting me. I know your sweet mama probably badgered you into it."

He had the grace to blush. "Not a problem."

She took the seat across from Alex and glanced at the plastic menu. "It smells so good in here. What are you having?"

A bony woman with orange frizzy hair hanging past her shoulders stopped at their booth. She held a coffee pot in her hand. "You folks ready to order?"

Sierra grinned. "Coffee, please. Then one of everything."

The woman's lips curled downward. "Pardon?"

"I was kidding. Can I get your Country Ham and Egg Breakfast? With the eggs over easy?"

The woman nodded and moved her attention to Alex. "What about you?"

"Coffee and the All-Star Special with hashbrowns for me."

After pouring coffee for each of them, she yelled the order over to the cook and let them know it would be out as soon as possible.

Alex found himself relaxing with Sierra. She had a funny sense of humor and an easy-going temperament. No wonder Mom thought they'd hit it off.

Under different circumstances, he'd consider asking her on a proper date. But for some reason, he couldn't make the words come out.

After breakfast and working on a major lawn project, he pulled up at home. As soon as he stepped out of his truck, his chest filled with laughter.

All the plants had been moved around on his porch. A single sheet of paper containing the words *"I'm not sorry"* hung on the front door.

Chapter 23

Frankie relaxed in the corner of the sectional, curling her legs beneath her. She opened her new planner and got busy laying out her days for the rest of the month. Clarence Little had finished updating all but one of the small cabins.

He'd also started a crew on updates in the main cabin. After a thorough inspection, she'd decided it needed more than a minor overhaul.

Alex would be handling the yardwork, so all Frankie needed to do was finish painting the main cabin after Clarence's crew cleared out. And handle the decorations. And figure out a plan for the Christmas festivities.

Her tongue poked the inside of her cheek. She needed help. Lottie, whatever her last name was, had seemed to honestly want the work. Should she be judging the woman, or should she give her a chance?

Lunelle Baldridge and Rhnae, along with several church members, had volunteered to help. Frankie appreciated it, but she really needed someone to help on a daily basis.

Could Lottie be that person? Frankie couldn't pinpoint what, but something about the woman pulled Frankie to her.

Before she talked herself out of it, she dialed her number and asked that she stop by for an interview.

Vandon set a glass of lemon ice water on the table beside Frankie. "You need to drink more water."

Frankie chugged water from the straw and smiled. "Yes, I do. Thank you." She set the water down and bit her bottom lip. "I have a woman I met at the cabins the other day on the way over for an interview. I need help with the Christmas camp."

Vandon pushed the sleeves of her sweatshirt up. Her wardrobe was predictable. So far, Frankie had seen her wearing dresses that reminded Frankie of hospital gowns or matching sweatsuits. Even in the heat. "I can help you."

"Oh, I know that, and I appreciate you. I still think it's a good idea to hire someone."

"Suit yourself." Vandon meandered down the hall, steadily mumbling something to herself.

Frankie winced. Hopefully, Vandon's feelings weren't hurt.

A little while later, the doorbell rang.

Lottie stood on the other side. "Hello, Lottie." Frankie stepped aside, motioning into the room. "Come on in."

Both Lottie's hands wrapped around her purse strap so tight they seemed ready to burst. "Thank you for calling me."

"No problem. Have a seat." Frankie reclaimed her spot on the sectional. "Would you like something to drink?"

Vandon appeared and strode into the kitchen. "Tea or water?"

She didn't even give the woman a chance to answer. That's one thing Frankie loved about Vandon. She took charge.

After lowering herself into a chair, Lottie smiled at Vandon. "Tea sounds good if it's sweet. Thank you."

Vandon cocked her head as she handed Lottie the tea. "Do I know you?"

Lottie shifted in her seat before taking the tea. "I don't think so."

After giving Lottie a few more looks, Vandon walked into the kitchen. "I'll give you two some privacy."

Lottie watched Vandon slip out the back door. "Look, I don't have a resume or a long line of references. I've not had a good job in over seven years."

Frankie tapped her ink pen on her chin. "What did you do before?"

She swallowed a sip of tea as she set the glass on a coaster on the side table. "I spent three years working at a hotel before I relapsed two years ago."

"Tell me about your duties while you worked at the hotel." If she'd managed to keep the job for three years, she must've been a good worker.

"Well, I started out as a front desk attendant before they promoted me to Assistant Manager after my first year."

"So, what happened?" Frankie looked at her paper. Maybe she shouldn't have asked such a personal question. Looking up, she caught Lottie's eyes scanning Frankie as if she were Lottie's last hope. "I'm sorry, you don't have to answer that."

"I ran into an old friend. He said he'd changed, so I let him back into my life." Her voice came out dull. Frankie glimpsed Lottie's eyes, and it was like she'd been sucker punched. "That was the worst mistake I could've made."

"Where is this friend?"

A frown etched the sides of her mouth. "Dead."

Chapter 24

If Frankie had thought June was hot, then July was a scorcher. Thank goodness they had the cool Gulf water to enjoy.

She pulled her hair into a messy bun and slathered turquoise paint on a brush. Lottie wrung a soapy rag out and started scrubbing the sawdust out of the new kitchen cabinets.

Over the past few weeks, they'd fallen into a routine of cleaning, visiting local businesses for donations, and recruiting vendors. The contractor had finished almost all the major repairs, so now it was time to focus on the design piece.

The only bad thing was that Frankie still didn't know how to turn the camp into a Christmas Wonderland like Daddy wanted.

Some people from the church should be there any minute to brainstorm. It was time to call out for help. A knock sounded from the front door.

As if she conjured them up, Gareth and Keatyn Davenport stood on the other side. Gareth smiled, revealing deep dimples. "Put us to work, boss."

Frankie's mouth dripped into a half-smile. "I need to work your brains today. I have no idea how to make this place a Christmas Wonderland."

Keatyn exchanged hugs with Frankie and then Lottie. "Between all of us, I bet we can come up with a great plan."

A car door slammed. Lottie glanced out the window before turning eyes full of unshed tears on Frankie. "Please excuse me. I don't feel well at all." She bolted through the back of the cabin.

Frankie followed her, but Lottie seemed to be running a marathon. She went inside the cabin she'd been staying in. Frankie stopped, staring after her a second before heading back the way she'd come. Lottie was a grown woman with an addiction. Maybe she just needed time to process everything.

Vandon, Lunelle, and Rhnae, along with a few other church members, had joined Gareth and Keatyn inside the main cabin.

A few more car doors slammed before Alex walked in with a woman Frankie didn't recognize. Confidence oozed from the woman with her blonde hair and perfect face. She could easily be a social media influencer.

Frankie plastered on a big smile and tried to ignore the way her stomach lurched. She approached the influencer wannabe with her hand stuck out. "Hello, I'm Frankie."

A smile breezed across the woman's lips as she embraced Frankie's hand. "Sierra Wood. Nice to meet you."

After introductions, the group followed Frankie into the dining area. Apparently, Sierra had already been to church and met Keatyn and Gareth. Good for her.

The dining area was big enough to hold around a hundred people. Most of the tables had been removed, but a few had been cleaned.

Vandon pulled a few bottles of water out of an ice chest. "Grab a water, people. It's too hot not to."

They settled around the tables with their waters.

Frankie took a swig of hers and bit her lip. "Thank you all for coming. We're getting close to having the major repairs completed. Now we need help figuring out how to make this place a Christmas Wonderland."

Rhnae's face lit up. "Are you bringing in fake snow?"

Alex followed suit. "I think that's a great idea, Rhnae. I'll look into it."

Lunelle nodded in agreement. "Will the kids be able to participate in the vendor booths? Ronnie and I have a few in our household that are very crafty."

Again, Alex spoke up. "Yes. That's something Larry and I discussed. We wanted to give the kids something to work on and look forward to."

Frankie bit her tongue to keep from making a smart remark. He worked on this with Daddy. While she was kept in the dark.

They spent the next hour brainstorming and making notes. Lottie had texted Frankie, saying she was taking a nap. Odd, but okay.

Before they left, Keatyn invited Sierra to an upcoming church outing at Fort Pickens.

Later that night, Frankie curled up on the sectional in the dark. She pointed a laser at Alex's house, doing her best to get it to shine through his windows.

The light clicked on. "What in the world are you doing?" Vandon looked at Frankie with her head cocked.

Vandon probably thought Frankie was a nutjob.

She laid the laser on the table. "I was just…"

"Just what?" Her mom voice hit Frankie hard. She hadn't heard that tone since that day at Lake Des Arc with Melody.

Frankie avoided making eye contact with her. "Trying to get on Alex's nerves so much he decides I'm unstable and takes on the property without me."

Vandon burst into laughter. "Oh my. If I were in your shoes, I'd be trying to figure out a way to date him, not run him off."

Without another word, she headed down the hall, steadily snickering.

At Frankie's expense.

Chapter 25

Deep in thought, Frankie didn't hear Lottie enter the office in the main cabin. She was too busy trying to figure out how to keep the same old furniture that had been left behind to save money.

Maybe all it needed was a good scrubbing, and it would work just fine. The maroon chair did look almost as good as new, save a few rusty spots by the wheels.

She looked up when Lottie cleared her throat. "Good morning, Lottie. How are you feeling?"

The question left Lottie blinking like she was trying to think of the correct answer. Finally, her shoulder bobbed. "I'm feeling a bit better." She darted her eyes toward the window, seeming to stare at the cluster of palm trees scattered about. "Do you know if anyone is coming here today to help?"

"Nope. Vandon has an appointment, and everyone else is working or in school. Looks like you'll be stuck with me all day." The same cat Vandon had petted strolled into the office. Frankie's lips edged up at the corners. "Well, me and him, anyway."

Lottie picked the cat up and hugged it to her face. A quiet laugh sprinkled the air. "How'd you get in here, Dreamy?"

Frankie cocked her head as a memory of Mama's laughter pranced across her mind. She swallowed the thoughts of Mama and bunched her mouth into a pucker. "Dreamy?"

Color whooshed up Lottie's neck. "He reminds me of a Dreamsicle. You know, the orange and white ice cream bars?"

Dreamy hopped out of Lottie's arms and jumped into the other office chair.

The slight laugh morphed into a fit of chuckles. "That's hilarious. And creative." Frankie's tone changed to a more serious one. "You keep that up, and the Christmas Camp will turn out great and Christmasy."

Lottie laced her fingers together as the color from her neck landed on her cheeks. "I appreciate you saying that."

How Lottie laced her fingers together reminded Frankie of how Mama used to lace her own fingers together. Thinking of Mama sparked a strong desire to help the woman standing in front of her. She just had to figure out how.

"I meant it." Frankie lifted herself out of the chair and took a step toward Lottie. "I think you are a lot more creative than you realize."

Heartbreak reverberated from her smile. "I've been a worthless human being most of my life."

"It looks to me like you're doing your best to change." Frankie laid her hand on Lottie's shoulder. "That has to count for something."

Lottie inclined her head to one side. "I wish my daughter thought like that."

Her hand tensed as she stepped away from Lottie. "You have a daughter?"

"I do." Lottie swallowed and looked at the brown tile floor, her eyes welling with tears. "She got taken away from me a couple of years ago."

Frankie's heart clenched as she stared at Lottie. Something about this woman drew Frankie to her. Maybe because Lottie's life was more pitiful than her own. Whatever it was, she didn't want to see Lottie in pain. "Hey, you don't have to talk about this with me right now."

Lottie nodded and closed her eyes a second before locking onto Frankie's gaze. "Thank you, Frankie."

"Let's head to town. I want to meet with Erma Dean over at the fruit stand. She wants to set up a booth at the Christmas Festive." Frankie jutted her brows up. "She also offered to donate some canned vegetables and jams."

Later that evening, Frankie scooped up a package before skipping inside her home. A bubble of excitement hit Frankie as she pulled out a knife to open the box. She'd been waiting forever for this package.

If what she had planned for the night didn't force Alex to sell out, she didn't know what would.

After sliding a pair of gloves on, she pulled a yellowish Durian Fruit out of the package and laid it on the counter, careful to avoid the spikes.

One of the chefs who traveled around the world eating disgusting food labeled this fruit as the thirteenth nastiest, stinkiest food he'd ever eaten. She hoped the fruit lived up to its reputation.

At nightfall, Frankie glanced at Alex's. Several lights shined, and his truck sat in the driveway.

Good.

She fired up the gas grill in the backyard and set a pot of water on the burner. After pointing a shop fan directly at the neighbors, she found her gloves and a face mask and got to work trying to cut the fruit open.

After one cut, a smell Frankie compared to a dead rat forced itself down her nose. Thankfully, Vandon had a dinner date with a friend from church, or she'd probably have a fit.

It took her ten solid minutes to get the fruit cut. Even the mask she wore couldn't keep the smell of rotten tuna mixed with month-old garbage and something dead from assaulting her nostrils.

She gagged and briefly considered rethinking her plan.

But nobody had ever called Frankie a quitter.

After dumping the fruit, shell, and all in the pan of water, she ran to the side of the yard and lost her dinner.

"What is this madness?" Vandon held her hand over her nose and mouth. "Are you boiling something using sewage instead of water?"

Instead of answering, she placed her hands on her legs, losing what little food was left in her stomach.

This had to be the most terrible idea ever.

Chapter 26

Alex shook a generous amount of garlic powder on top of a slew of other spices and mixed them into the lean ground beef. He had a few minutes before Gareth got there with his twin brother, Cody, and Alex's good buddy, Alvin Griffin.

They planned on grilling and having a Bible study.

Alvin, who happened to be Gareth's brother-in-law, was also Alex's best friend. Alvin had moved to Tampa the year before, so they didn't get to see each other as often as they used to.

Keatyn and Alvin's wife, Sylvia, had planned a girls' night, so the men decided to take advantage and have a men's night.

After patting the burgers out, he stuck them in the fridge and headed out back to fire up the charcoal grill.

As soon as he opened the back door, a stench he could only describe as putrid rotting meat forced itself into his nostrils and down his throat.

Bile pooled inside his stomach. He walked inside, slamming the door shut with his foot. He opened the fridge and gulped down some chocolate milk directly from the jug.

It didn't help.

He walked the three steps to the sink and turned the cold water on, putting his head under the faucet.

His guests burst through the front door. He could only tell Gareth and Cody apart by their hair length. Cody kept his in a buzz cut, whereas Gareth's had a little length on top.

Cody leaned on the sink beside Alex, holding his stomach, doubled over in as laughter rippled from his throat. "Why does your neighbor hate you?"

Alex shook his hair out and looked at Cody with a blank expression on his face. "What are you talking about?"

Alvin and Gareth both had their shirts covering their noses. Alvin pointed out the back door. "Come outside. You'll see what Cody's talking about."

Alex's stomach rolled, and he shook his head. "I don't think I can."

Always the one to look for the good in people, Gareth spoke up. "There has to be an explanation."

Cody had laughed so much that he now had tears streaming down his face.

Alex couldn't stand it. He had to know what it was they were talking about.

He covered his nose the best he could before stepping outside. The grill in Frankie's backyard held a pot of the most horrible thing Alex could imagine, and a shop fan blew it right at Alex's house.

Loud voices coming from the front of the house reached Alex's ears. He and Gareth took off in the same direction while Cody and Alvin headed toward the grill.

Their neighbor, Mrs. Pinkerton, sat half-leaning out of a golf cart, poking her finger in Frankie's face. "I don't care how sorry you are. You've stunk the whole neighborhood up, girl!"

Vandon kept a cool tone as she tried to calm Mrs. Pinkerton down. "Come on, Viola, you know how it is for young folks."

Her mouth spread into a stern line. "I don't care about none of that. Get that rotten whatever it is taken to the dumpster. Now!"

After hitting Frankie with a nasty look, she drove away.

Alex ought to chew her a new one. After everything she'd been doing to make his life hard, this last stunt also had to be for his benefit. He stomped past Vandon, ready to let Frankie have it.

As soon as she looked at him, tears started to fall. His anger deflated as quickly as it had come. "What is it? Do you like eating rotten onions for supper?"

Alex saw the small smile that graced her perfect lips just before she tried to hide her face with her arm.

Cody held up a package. "It's Durian fruit."

Alex tore his gaze away from Frankie. "Never heard of it." Cody tried to hand Alex the package, but he held his hands up. "No, thank you."

"Vandon, you can go to the store or somewhere while I clean this up." Frankie slogged her way toward the backyard.

Alex blocked her way and pointed at Vandon. "You get in that beautiful Camaro with Miss Vandon and go to the beach or something. I'll take care of this."

Her eyes doubled in size, but she shook her head. "I'm the one who did this. I should be the one to clean it up." Her head dropped, and she avoided his stare. "I'm sorry."

Vandon walked up to Frankie and grasped her forearm. Alex met her gaze and nodded his head in the driveway's direction. "Vandon, will you please get her to go?"

She nodded as she steered Frankie toward the Camaro. Vandon settled Frankie in the passenger's seat and, within seconds, zoomed out of the drive.

Even though Frankie had just tried to poison him with whatever kind of fruit that was, he couldn't stop his heart from pounding and every part of his being igniting a fire in his soul.

For a woman who pretended she couldn't stand him.

Chapter 27

Never in her life had Frankie acted so childish. Selfish. Hateful. The list could go on and on.

She ignored the churning in her stomach and rang the doorbell.

Thankfully the stench had dissipated overnight. But her embarrassment? Well, it had not. More like grown into a mountain.

The bright blue sunny sky lifted her spirits a little as she waited for the door to open. At least the weather seemed willing to cooperate for the church outing she'd agreed to attend at Fort Pickens.

She hadn't been there since she was eleven or twelve. So, today had to be a good day.

Alex appeared on the other side of the door. His red hair dripping water on his light blue T-shirt and the look on his face left Frankie at odds with how to start the conversation.

She twiddled with the end of her light pink and blue striped shirt. She opened and closed her mouth several times before deciding what to say. "I'm sorry for how I've treated you."

His eyebrows shot up, but a car door shut behind her before he could answer. Frankie half expected Alvin Griffin to be standing there. Instead, the Sierra lady walked up the sidewalk. Disappointment and another emotion she didn't care to feel coursed through her veins.

She pressed her teeth together to keep from screaming. Why did that woman have to interrupt their conversation when Frankie had finally worked the nerve up to apologize?

Frankie took inventory of Sierra's full face of makeup, straight hair, sporty white shorts, yellow top, and white sandals and found herself lacking. She'd never wished she'd taken a moment to at least put on some mascara so hard in her life.

Sierra flashed a huge grin at Alex. "Good morning." Her eyes raked over Frankie as she rubbed her fingers under her nose. "I hope I'm not too early."

Too early?

Yes, you're too early.

Alex stepped out onto the porch. "Not at all. I'm ready to head out." He smiled at Sierra and then Frankie. "You wanna ride with us to Fort Pickens?"

"Thank you, but no." Frankie's tone couldn't have been any sweeter had she swallowed a cup of honey.

He poked his head back inside, grabbed his keys, and then clicked the door closed "You are going, right?"

Sierra seemed to feel out of place as she checked her watch for the third time.

Frankie moved her eyes from Sierra to Alex. If only she had waited a little longer to apologize. Like six hours. "I was planning on it. I think Keatyn would kill me if I didn't."

A beeping horn sounded from the road. Mrs. Pinkerton shook her fist as she drove by. Frankie couldn't stop the grin that lit her face, but she quickly bit her bottom lip. It really wasn't funny.

Okay, maybe it was a little bit funny.

Alex's smile matched Frankie's. He coughed in his hand and landed gleaming eyes on Frankie. "Vandon can ride with us, too, if she's going."

An almost uncomfortable sensation curdled Frankie's stomach. It was like she and Alex had just shared a secret, special moment.

One that the influencer wannabe Sierra had no part in.

Heat settled in Frankie's face. She had no desire to ride with them. "No, she's not."

He raised his brow and slightly cocked his head. "After what you just said, I figured you'd ride with us."

Guess he decided to go for blood. Maybe she should think of riding with them as her punishment for the fruit incident. "All right. Let me grab my purse."

By the time they reached Fort Pickens, Frankie had worked herself into a tizzy. She'd regretted jumping into the back seat of Alex's truck as soon as she did it. But why? She didn't want to sit up front by him anyway.

Right?

Fort Pickens held so much history Frankie couldn't decide where to go first. She passed a cannon and made her way to a tunnel. Worn brick lined the floors and tunnel-like walls. What an amazing thing it was to be able to see this place as it was back then.

After walking through a great deal of the fort, Frankie stopped along the trail. She read about the sixteen Apache Prisoners who had been imprisoned at Fort Pickens in the year 1886. A chill traveled her spine, knowing Geronimo had walked across the same place she stood. Maybe even the exact spot.

Alex touched her elbow. "We got interrupted earlier, so I failed to say I accept your apology."

Trails of shivers traveled from Alex's touch all the way to her fingertips. She rubbed the spot and lifted her lips into a half smile. "It's okay. As long as we're good."

"I hope we're more than good." His tone came out silky smooth.

Keatyn stopped behind them and eyeballed Frankie with a raised brow. "Hey, Frankie, can I talk to you for a minute?"

"Sure, what's up?" She prayed her voice didn't sound like a squeaky toy to anyone else.

Keatyn grasped Frankie's hand and waited until Alex got out of earshot before she spoke. "You two have a spark, big time."

With everything that had transpired since last night, Frankie wasn't sure her spine could stiffen any more than it already had.

Wrong.

"Who? Me and Alex? Oh no."

Keatyn's eyes glimmered, reminding Frankie of the turquoise water under the bridge going to Destin. "Oh, yes."

Maybe it would be better to ignore Keatyn. Pretend she hadn't said that. But from the way Keatyn still gripped Frankie's hand, she wouldn't let that happen. A light bulb went off – why not state the obvious?

"He brought a date."

Keatyn's little girl, Lily, jumped up and down, trying to get her attention. Keatyn waved and yelled that she'd be there in just a minute. "He is *not* on a date. Patsy asked him to spend time showing Sierra around. She just moved here for work."

Well, that could change things. Frankie rubbed her bottle of water along her neck. "Patsy, as in Alex's mom?"

"Yep. But don't get me wrong. He likes Sierra. It's just that his eyes don't light up like they do with you."

A tremor tickled her belly as her heart stuttered in her chest. "You must be imagining things."

"I'm rarely wrong about these things. Plus, I think Sierra needs to meet my brother-in-law, Cody." She put a finger up to Lily, who had started back in yelling for her mama. "Come on, let's go check out the jail cells before Lily loses what little patience she has left."

"Well, I do think you're wrong about Alex being interested in me." She kept a slow and steady stride as she walked away with Keatyn, but her insides screamed about like they did ten years ago.

Alex came to a halt ahead and locked a grin on Frankie. She swallowed and gave a curt nod. That's all she could manage, with her insides flipping around like she'd just gotten out of a dryer cycle.

Chapter 28

After spending the past hour exploring the trails behind the cabins, Frankie plopped down on one of the benches Gareth and his brother, Cody, had built along the trails.

They had several throughout the trails and a couple at the edge of the lake. Having places to rest should make it more attractive, especially to elderly folks. At least, that's what Vandon had announced.

She sucked down some of her Strawberry Frappe and wiped the whipped cream off her chin. Dark gray clouds scooted across the sky, reminding Frankie of the day they buried Daddy. She wished he was here to hug her and give her advice on what to do about her feelings for Alex.

A bird let out a chirp, bringing Frankie's attention to the tree. It had a red cap and black and white horizontal striped wings that any master artist could've carefully painted.

After scoping Frankie out for a few minutes, it flew off the branch and landed on the ground. It immediately started pecking at something Frankie couldn't see. It pecked and then scanned its surroundings. This went on for several minutes.

Bird calls sounded all around Frankie, giving her a feeling of peace that she hadn't known in quite a long time. She tugged the long-sleeved sweater off, revealing a plain white t-shirt. October in Pensacola felt like August back home.

Melody's name lit across her phone screen with a FaceTime request. Frankie grinned.

"Hi, bestie."

"I miss you." Melody's face filled the entire screen.

Frankie poked her bottom lip out. "I miss you, too."

"How are you doing with the cabins?" Melody leaned back, revealing she was sitting in her car.

"Oh, they're coming along. It's just..."

"What?"

"You're not driving, are you?"

"Of course not, silly. I'm waiting for Raines. What's wrong?"

"Nothing."

"Liar. What's going on?"

The bird flew off, landing on the same tree limb as before. Frankie sighed. "I think I have feelings for Alex."

"Feelings of....?"

"You know, but he's been dating someone else the past few weeks."

"Oh, Frankie. I hate that."

They talked a few more minutes before a car pulled into the drive, interrupting their conversation. "Hey, I better go see who's here."

"Okay. Love you."

"Love you, too. And thanks for listening."

Frankie jogged to the main cabin, only to walk into a screaming match. All four people in the cabin stood around the pool table in the game room.

Rhnae tensed and gave Frankie a dirty look. Took Frankie back to the first time she ever saw her. "How could you hire this woman and not tell me?"

Frankie cut her eyes at Lottie and screwed her face up. "What do you mean?"

Lunelle grabbed Rhnae by the arm and started toward the door. "Lottie is Rhnae's mother."

"Mother?" A whoosh of betrayal coursed through Frankie's veins. She hated being used more than anything.

Lunelle paused at the door. "You didn't know?"

"No. I promise." Frankie looked from Rhnae to Lottie. "But I will get to the bottom of this."

After nudging Rhnae out ahead of herself, Lunelle glared at Lottie. "I'm sorry for what you're going through, but my priority is Rhnae, as yours should be. It's best we go."

Lunelle disappeared through the front door behind Rhnae. That's when Frankie looked at Vandon. Her face seemed haggard, like she'd been through something.

"Please tell me what's going on. Now."

Vandon dropped her head. "This is Lottie McKenna."

"I know her name, Vandon." Frankie stared at Lottie. "What I need to know is why you lied."

Tears flowed from Lottie's eyes. "I told you I have a daughter."

"But I had no idea it was Rhnae." Frankie face palmed herself. "Now I know why you always ran away when she's around."

Lottie twisted the end of her blue and white striped t-shirt that she had balled up in her hand. "I'm sorry."

Vandon put her hands up. "That's not even the tip of the iceberg, Frankie. How many McKenna's have you known in your life?"

Lottie's cries melted into sobs. She moved across the room and stopped by Frankie, who stood in the doorway. "I wanted to tell you."

A chilling dread pooled in Frankie's stomach. The chill threatened to turn into a flaming fire as she narrowed her eyes at Lottie. "Tell me what?"

"Your mother was my sister."

The burning tingles Frankie had fought overpowered her as they consumed her body and mind. "Get out."

"Please, don't." Lottie reached her hand out only to drop it when Frankie walked away.

"I said, get out. You're fired." Frankie hit the doorframe with her shoulder as she stomped out of the room.

She never wanted to see that woman again.

Chapter 29

Drops of rain splattered Alex's windshield as he drove toward the cabins. His mind whirled with thoughts of Frankie. Even though she'd stopped trying to buy him out, she still showed no interest in him.

What could he be doing wrong? She still liked him, so what kept her from showing it?

An incoming call from Sierra took his mind off Frankie, at least for a few minutes. Sierra was a beautiful and wonderful woman, and a part of him wanted her to steal his heart.

The fact she hadn't remained a mystery since she'd made her intentions clear the past couple of weeks. Ever since then, Alex had pulled away. He'd told her he wasn't looking for a relationship from the beginning. She just hadn't listened.

That wasn't his fault.

Right?

Alex clicked the wipers on high as the rain poured harder. It looked like a woman on the side of the road up ahead. Surely, his eyes were playing tricks on him. He picked up his speed and pulled over when he reached her, careful not to splash water on her.

He rolled the passenger window down and screwed his mouth up. "Lottie? Why are you walking down the road? Get in."

She slid into the seat with her teeth chattering. "I'm getting water everywhere."

"Don't worry about that." He flipped the seat warmer on. "Let's get to the cabin so you can dry off."

She grabbed the door handle like she was prepared to jump. "Please don't do that."

He pressed on the brake in case she opened the door. "Why not? What's going on?"

"I've messed everything up. Again." Her face sagged as her grip on the door handle tightened.

He kept one hand on the steering wheel but raised the other one like he surrendered. "Tell me what's got you so upset."

Between sobs, she filled Alex in, leaving no detail out.

A heaviness seemed to cover his chest. Frankie had fired Lottie without even allowing her to give her reasons for not saying anything. "That explains why you left. But why are you walking in the rain? Where's your car?"

"It died." She put her hands over the vent. "I pulled off the road, so it should be fine until tomorrow."

He coasted down the road, careful to avoid a couple of holes along the way. He made a mental note to have them filled in. "Let's make sure really quick."

"I don't want to put you out." She paused and looked out the window a few seconds. "But I could use a ride back to my car to get my bag and then to the shelter."

He knitted his eyebrows together. "The shelter?"

"Yeah, they should be able to put me up a night or so until I can figure things out." She pointed at a pull-off. "There's my Ford."

When Lottie got out, Alex wasted no time calling Gareth. "Gareth. We have a situation with Lottie McKenna." He filled Gareth in as quickly as possible.

"Can you and maybe Keatyn meet us at the Comfort Inn?"

"Yes, let me call Keatyn's Uncle Rodney and have him meet us. He's the elder over benevolence."

"Thank you so much. I can't tell you how much I appreciate you."

A couple of hours later, Alex knocked on Frankie's front door.

Vandon pulled the door open, and her lips twitched downward. "Hey, Alex. Come on in."

Frankie blew her nose and opened bloodshot eyes full of what Alex would call regret. He ran a hand through his hair, trying to figure out what to say without sounding too mean.

She stood and marched over to the trash can, throwing the tissue away. "I guess you've heard what happened?"

One one hundred. Two two hundred. Three three hundred. "I saw Lottie walking down the road, sopping wet in the cold rain. So yeah, I heard."

"Why was she walking in the rain?" Her voice came out muffled. She kept her back to Alex, just standing in front of the trash can.

A sigh fell from his lips. "Didn't you fire her, or did she make that up?"

"I refuse to have a bald-faced liar working for me." Her voice rose, but she never moved from her spot.

Alex breathed out through his mouth, and his jaw clenched as he stared at Frankie, searching for the right words. "You have got to be kidding me. I never figured you to be such a selfish person."

Frankie whipped around. She stared at Alex for a split second with her mouth gaping open. "Don't you dare turn this around on me. That woman is to blame. Not me."

He took a couple of faltering steps in her direction. "Would your daddy be happy with the way you're acting? With the incorrigible way you're treating your own aunt?"

An acidic bark of laughter left Frankie as she closed the space between them. Their eyes battled as they stared one another down.

He hadn't been this close to Frankie in many years. Her face almost touched his. A mixture of mango and coconut drifted from her curls, encompassing his senses. For a moment, he imagined burying his fingers in those curls.

They stood silent and stiff, each daring the other to speak.

Vandon cleared her throat. "Frankie? Did you not hear the doorbell?"

Frankie answered Vandon, never once taking her eyes away from Alex. "I did not."

Melody Rodgers poked Frankie on the shoulder. "Not sure what's going on here, but you two need to take a breather."

Frankie whipped her head in Melody's direction. "What are you doing here?"

"We came to surprise you." Melody scrunched up her face as her shoulder bobbed. "Surprise."

Frankie narrowed her eyes at Alex before intertwining her arm with Melody's. After one last stony-faced look at Alex, they disappeared down the hallway without another word.

Alex had to get away from this place. From her. He spun around, locking eyes with Melody's husband, Raines. And another man he didn't recognize.

The man stepped forward, blocking Alex's path. "Who are you?"

Who was he? At the moment, he didn't know how to answer that question. Frankie's business partner? Her next-door neighbor? The man who loved her more than anything else in the world?

Wait a minute. Love? Where did that come from?

Could the feelings that have been driving him mad mean he was in love with Frankie?

Somehow, he answered the man even though the drum of his heart overtook everything else around him. "Alex Foster. Frankie's business partner." That would have to do. For now.

The man's gray eyes narrowed. "I'm Brayden Parker. Frankie's boyfriend."

Chapter 30

The visit with her friends turned out to be a nice distraction from the situation with Lottie. That woman had some nerve coming to work for Frankie.

You have to be the lowest of the low to look someone in the face and lie. Where had she been all Frankie's life? Mama had spent what seemed like years searching for her sister.

Until one day, she stopped searching. Frankie had once overheard her and Daddy talking about how Charlotte must be dead.

Charlotte. That's what Mama said her name was. Not that Frankie would've recognized Lottie in the first place, but the names were different. All she'd ever seen of the woman was a couple of pictures from when Mama was a teenager.

She thought of Lottie's laughter when the cat, Dreamy, had chased the laser lights Frankie shined on the wall one night when they worked late.

Her laughter had reminded Frankie of the way Mama used to laugh. She'd chalked it up to a coincidence.

Ha. Lies. Manipulation.

Several times, Lottie reminded Frankie of something she hadn't been able to put her finger on. Now it all made sense.

Heat ran up her neck. Oh no, she had to think of something else, or her day would be ruined. And there's no way she'd give Lottie that much power over her.

The best way to take her mind off that situation was to think of something else. Like her friends coming when they found out how upset she was over Lottie. She still couldn't believe they flew to Pensacola for one night.

Especially Brayden.

That man confused her like no other. His looks had always caused Frankie's heart to flutter, but he'd never tried to date her. Until she moved. What was up with that?

Could it be that he hadn't made a move because she worked for his sister at The Lily Pad Boutique? Now that she no longer worked there, he proba-bly felt free to pursue a relationship.

He'd been very attentive at dinner and seemed to enjoy spending time with her last night. His face had lit up when she offered to let him spend the night at the cabin.

After giving them a tour of all the changes, Brayden and Raines both decided to bunk in one of the cabins while Melody spent the night with Frankie and Vandon.

Now that they had headed home, it was time for Frankie to gear up for a meeting with Alex. She recently spoke with Simon and a local financial advisor about turning the camp into a business. The location had everything one would need for church camps, school day trips, work events, and even weddings.

Alex would need to be on board, though. How could Daddy pair her with Alex like this? She didn't need a partner. Well, maybe financially, she did, but it could've been anyone else.

Realistically, she could live off Daddy's life insurance, her savings, and what Daddy had left her for the next several years, but she needed a job. A purpose.

The front door banging open interrupted Frankie's thoughts. Within seconds, Alex bounded into the office, his face a mask of worry.

Frankie jumped to her feet and scurried around the desk. Something had to be wrong. "What is it?"

He wiped his left hand down his mouth and closed the space between them. "Mrs. Pinkerton found Vandon on the ground. She was on her way to the hospital when I left to come here."

Her nostrils flared as anger mixed with worry swelled in her chest. "Why didn't you call me?"

"I called you at least five times." He stepped out of the office but kept talking like he knew Frankie would follow. "It kept going straight to voicemail. Figured I better drive over."

With a moan, she dug around in her purse for her phone as they walked. A black cell phone screen stared at her, mocking her. "It's dead."

Why did she always look like a fool around this man?

Once outside, Alex opened the passenger door to his truck. "Let me drive you to the hospital."

She opened her mouth to protest, but one look at her trembling hands changed her mind. "Okay."

They'd driven a few minutes when Frankie swallowed her pride and trained her gaze on Alex. "Look, I'm sorry for being hateful. It's just...if she's not okay, I don't know what I'll do."

He stared out the windshield for what seemed like ten minutes before he spoke when they pulled up to a red light. "I appreciate that." He glanced to the left before making a right-hand turn. "Just know that Vandon is a tough person. She's gonna be just fine. The Lord will take care of her. Many of us have been praying."

"Daddy made sure I have Vandon." She wrapped her arms around herself before locking her eyes on Alex's. "I can't lose her."

It was like Alex read her need for human contact as he reached across the seat and grasped her hand. "Pray, Frankie. Pray and have faith and trust in God's will."

By the time they made it to the emergency room, Gareth was already there. He walked up to them and offered Frankie a hug. "Her blood sugar levels bottomed out, but they have her hooked up to an IV now. Thankfully, Mrs. Pinkerton saw her hit the ground and called 911 immediately."

The tight funnel of air stuck in Frankie's lungs seeped out. "Thank the Lord." Alex had been right. Praying and then placing her trust in God had calmed her anxious heart.

Gareth nodded and then excused himself to speak to someone he knew.

Alex squeezed her hand before wrapping his arms around her. "When you said you were sorry earlier, I should've said I'm sorry, too."

His soft tone rattled her bones. "For what?"

He leaned back and met her gaze. "Being less than nice sometimes."

That earned him a grin. "How about we start over?"

He nodded. "You've got yourself a deal."

Chapter 31

Beeps from the air fryer and the aroma of crunchy Italian breadcrumbs mixed with olive oil woke Frankie from her nap on the sectional. Scrambling to make it to the kitchen before Mrs. Pinkerton heard it, she pulled the tray out.

Her lips slipped downward. The zucchini chips didn't look like they did on the internet. It looked like she'd sliced them up and thrown them in the fryer with breadcrumbs on the side. The ones online had a crispy crust. At least she'd made a practice round.

Why hadn't she stuck with the pot roast? She surprised herself when a laugh sprang from her chest.

Why should it, though? She had plenty to be happy about. For one, Vandon would be released from the hospital after the doctor signed off on her papers later today.

Oddly, she'd insisted that Frankie not come pick her up. Said she had a ride and wouldn't take no for an answer. Frankie bet it was Mrs. Pinkerton. Now that her ankle had healed, she zoomed all over the place.

After checking on the pot roast, Frankie settled onto her spot by the window. She pulled out an old photo album and stared at her last photo with her parents. Instead of the deep pain she normally felt, a sparkle lifted her heart.

The sound of a weed eater drifted through the open window. A spasm of tingles racked Frankie's stomach, stopping at her throat.

Alex.

Their talk at the hospital had eased her mind, but she needed to clear the air completely. She continued to look through the photo album until she no longer heard the weed eater. After pulling her curls into a bun, she headed out the back door.

Alex knelt beside the fence just as she stepped around it. He stood, slapping a ball cap against his leg. Lines pulled at the corners of his mouth. "I hope I didn't wake you up with the weed-eating."

She flung her hands out, stopping a few feet from where he stood. "Oh no. I've been awake practicing my cooking skills for supper."

"Gareth said Vandon will be coming home to-day." He took a swig of water before walking up the porch steps, lowering himself onto the swing. He patted the seat beside him.

A gush of nerves attempted to overtake Frankie. Pushing them aside, she plopped onto the swing as far away from Alex as possible. "Yes, I'm so thankful."

He anchored his gaze to hers. "What brings you over?"

The look in his eyes sent her blood pumping overtime. She rubbed the back of her neck and broke eye contact. The whirling ceiling fan caught her attention. "I was hoping you'd tell me what happened with Lottie."

He pushed his feet down, setting the swing in motion, and filled her in on what happened when he picked Lottie up. He ended with, "The elders put Lottie up in the hotel down the road from the church so she wouldn't have to go to the homeless shelter."

A bloom of heat lit her neck. She hadn't even thought about Lottie's situation when she made her leave the cabin. Selfish wasn't a strong enough word to describe Frankie right now.

Hateful? Nope, not strong enough.

Uncaring? Not strong enough.

"Hey." Alex's soft voice and the heat from his hand on her shoulder snapped Frankie out of her fog.

He gathered her in his arms as spasms of tears racked her shoulders. Her chest constricted as she let the years of anguish flow as Alex held her.

The tight ball scrunched between her lungs that had been her constant companion since the day she buried Daddy seemed to loosen. She leaned back, mere inches from his face. The remnant of watermelon candy made Frankie's mouth water as Alex's breath tickled her cheek.

Could he possibly want to kiss her? No, he offered comfort, and that was it. No sense in letting her mind run wild when this was nothing but a passing moment. Even so, the heat from his hands burned her arms like hot coal.

The wind kicked up, letting them know a storm would be there soon. The half-shut storm door clicked out of place, banging against the house. Frankie let out a yelp, and Alex's lips lifted a notch.

Frankie scrambled to her feet, her heart gunning into overdrive. "I'm such a selfish, inconsiderate human being."

"I believe you were in shock." He stood, stopping directly in front of her. "Finding out Lottie is your mama's sister and didn't tell you had to be a hard pill to swallow."

A gray cloud covered the sky, and rain spattered against the awning.

Goosebumps lit Frankie's arms, and she shivered. "I couldn't believe it. For a minute, I thought she made the whole story up."

"What are you gonna do about it?"

A ray of sunshine peeked through the rain clouds, giving a small section of the sky a look of mystery. "What would you suggest?"

He leaned against the side of the house. His demeanor held a look of peace that Frankie longed for in her own life. "I'd suggest starting with prayer."

She closed her eyes for a moment, allowing the pattering of the rain to settle her mind. "What should I pray for?"

"I can't tell you exactly, but I'd start by praying for a stronger relationship with the Lord." He took her hand and gently rubbed her knuckles. "Frankie, you need to learn to lean on Him for all things. Pray for His will to be done with Lottie, Rhnae, you, and anything else weighing on your mind."

"You're right. I'll start by praying, then I'm going to bring Lottie over and talk things out." As soon as she said it, a weight lifted. Her mouth shifted to a smile, one that Alex returned.

"I know that she's been with Keatyn today." He let go of her hand, leaving a warmth behind. "You should text her and see."

After texting back and forth, Lottie agreed to stop by in an hour. Frankie blew out a breath, happy the ball was rolling with Lottie, yet worried about what she'd say to her.

Mrs. Pinkerton sped by on her golf cart, not sparing a glance at them. She stopped at her mailbox and got out, holding a black terrier.

Frankie's brow furrowed. "I need to speak to her real quick. Wanna come?"

Alex nodded. They stepped off the porch into the sprinkles of rain and made their way to Mrs. Pinkerton's yard.

Frankie waved. "Mrs. Pinkerton, are you the one picking Vandon up from the hospital?"

She shook her head, and her mouth flipped to a frown. "Nope. I would've been happy to, but she had other plans."

Frankie put her hand out to the terrier, and it snapped at her. She jerked her hand back with a furrowed brow. "What other plans?"

A glimmer of a smile twinkled across Mrs. Pinkerton's face, and Frankie saw a beauty in her she'd never noticed. She itched to tell her she needed to smile more often but decided against it.

"You'll have to wait and see, now, won't you?" She shut her mailbox and climbed back into her golf cart, driving toward the back of her house.

Alex shrugged. "That was an odd conversation."

Frankie kept her gaze on Mrs. Pinkerton until she disappeared. The sky darkened, and a shot of rain hit them fast and hard. Alex grabbed her hand, and they ran to his front porch, laughing all the way.

Chapter 32

The blinds hit the window with a ding as Frankie scurried to the front door. She opened it in time to see Lottie step out of Keatyn's gray Infiniti SUV. Keatyn waved before backing out of the driveway.

Lottie took a tentative step toward the front porch before pausing to take a few deep breaths. She must be as nervous as Frankie.

Frankie took a deep breath of her own and opened the door wide. "Thank you for agreeing to come over here."

She tugged at her black slacks as she climbed the steps. "Thanks for the invite."

Once inside, Frankie walked around the island. "Would you like a cup of coffee?"

"That sounds good." Lottie sat on the end of the sectional. "The rain has been chilly today."

Frankie brought two cups of coffee over and sat in the chair across from Lottie. "First off, I owe you an apology for the way I acted."

Lottie took a sip of her coffee and wrapped her hands around the mug. "I put you in an impossible situation. This is on me, not you, and I need your forgiveness."

Frankie took inventory of Lottie's movements. Now she knew why Lottie reminded her of someone on occasion. It was Mama. "Will you start by telling me why you kept your identity from me?"

"I figured you'd think I was after something." Pain flashed across her face. "Plus, who would want a drug addict for an aunt? I didn't want to embarrass you."

Frankie blew on her coffee before taking a sip. "Maybe it was my fault. It's not like I was the most welcoming person."

"No, it's my paranoia that caused our situation."

Frankie didn't know how to answer that. She'd lived a sheltered life and had no dealings with drugs. "What would you think about taking some time to get to know one another?"

Her lips formed a smile. "I'd be honored to get to know you, Frankie."

"Would you tell me where you've been my whole life?" Wouldn't Mama want her to give Lottie a chance? Hadn't Lottie's life been hard enough without Frankie putting her through the wringer over their situation?

"Let me start at the beginning. Me and Helen had such good parents. They loved us up until the day they died in the car accident." Her eyes took on a distant look like she'd been transported to another time. "We didn't have many close kin, so we got sent to a children's home. That's where Helen met Larry. He was such a good boy."

She took another drink of coffee before continuing.

"But I was another story. I fell in with a group of kids who hated the world. Before long, I hated the world, too."

Frankie lifted herself out of the chair and sat beside Lottie. "You don't have to tell me everything."

"I want to. We all have our closets, and mine's full. May as well get it all out at once. I hated everything, including your mama and daddy. I know now I was jealous. They tried to get me to stay away from the kids I was hanging with. That did nothing but make me want to hang with them more. Eventually, Helen's worst fear happened. I started taking meth." A sob fell from her chest, and Frankie rested her hand on top of Lottie's. "Within a month, I ran away and never saw Helen again. Even after I heard Granny's sister took Helen in, I stayed away. Drugs owned me."

She pulled a tissue from the box off the side table and blew her nose. "Frankie, my life has revolved around drugs and alcohol. I got off after I had Rhnae for a while, but it didn't last."

Frankie pulled her leg underneath her body and settled on a fluffy pillow. "Has Rhnae been with you the entire time?"

"Not the entire time. She's spent her life hopping from place to place. That is until I overdosed and went into the hospital. That's when she got taken away."

"What happened to make you get off the drugs this time?"

"This time, I've been fully clean for six months. I got off meth after overdosing, but I turned to alcohol for a few months after I lost Rhnae. Waking up in a pool of vomit in an alley was what it took to open my eyes."

"Wow. What does fully clean mean?"

"It means I haven't had any substance for six months. No alcohol, painkillers, cigarettes, or any illegal or legal drug."

"That's wonderful. So, what is your plan with Rhnae?" Maybe Frankie had a chance to help Lottie make things right with Rhnae. If she could do something for someone else, maybe, just maybe, things would start to fall into place in her own life.

"Well, first thing, I need to find a job and a place to stay, then I'm going to try to get her back home with me."

This chance Frankie had to help couldn't slip through her fingers. She had to do this in Mama's place. "Your old job and the cabin are yours. We just need to figure out how to get Rhnae home."

"We?"

"Yes. We're family, right?" Family. It struck Frankie. Daddy had sent her to Pensacola even when she didn't want to go, and this is where she'd found family. Daddy had been a man of faith, and Frankie had no doubt he'd prayed about the decisions before he made them.

Now she had family. Those who were blood kin and those who would be family no matter what.

They spent the next couple of hours making a dessert for dinner and one to take to Alex. Frankie confessed her feelings for him, and Lottie had the same sentiment as Vandon. She needed to date him instead of trying to get rid of him.

Laughter riddled Frankie over the look on Lottie's face after they burned a batch of cookies. The front door clicked shut, and Vandon walked inside, followed by Simon Wheeler.

"Simon? What are you doing here? And Vandon, who picked you up from the hospital?"

Vandon grinned when Simon took her arm, leading her to the recliner. "Simon is the one who picked me up."

"But why?" Frankie dipped her head to the side. "I could've picked you up."

Simon draped a coverlet over Vandon and kissed her hand.

Wait. Why would Simon kiss Vandon's hand?

A blush crept up Vandon's neck. "Simon's my beau, Frankie. He wanted to pick me up."

Chapter 33

After his morning prayer, Alex pulled his bright blue rain jacket on and grabbed his coffee thermos. He clicked the front door open and came face to face with Frankie.

She froze in place, looking like she'd just been caught with her hand in the cookie jar. Curly ringlets framed her face and hung to her shoulders, entwined in a thick side braid.

She pressed a basket in his hands. "These are for you."

He pulled the checkered towel aside to peek at the contents. A face-splitting grin appeared as he breathed in the aroma of chocolate goodness. "You bought me chocolate chip cookies?"

She returned his grin. "I made them."

He bit a chunk out of one and groaned. "Wow, this is good and still warm."

Alex couldn't tell if it was the orange rays breaking free from the sunrise causing Frankie's neck to pinken or if she was embarrassed.

She tugged a curl behind her ear. "I'm glad you like it. Lottie helped me make them."

"Lottie?" He stuffed half of the cookie in his mouth.

She nodded as sweet laughter sprinkled the air, causing Alex's heart to falter. He hadn't heard such a laugh since Frankie was a kid. "I'm heading to make sure the beach is safe for sea turtles. Wanna go with me?"

"I'd love to. Give me a second to grab my jacket and let Lottie know where I'm going."

On the way to the beach, Alex traded a glance with Frankie. "So, I take it you and Lottie worked things out?"

"We did." Her tone came off light, carefree even. "We've been up all night getting to know each other and baking random sweets."

"What kind of sweets? I'll volunteer my service as a taste tester."

"We have some diabetic-friendly brownies, a strawberry cake that is to die for, and, of course, the cookies."

"Yeah, I'll definitely apply for the taste tester position."

She grinned, and excitement emanated from her. "You'll never guess who picked Vandon up from the hospital."

"Gareth and Keatyn?"

"Nope."

His mouth scrunched up. "One of the elders?"

"Nope." She bit her bottom lip, and a half laugh came out. "You remember speaking to my attorney, Simon Wheeler?"

"I do. Are you telling me he picked her up?"

"Yes. Simon called the house phone one day looking for me when my cell went to voicemail, and Vandon answered. Apparently, they got to talking and really hit it off."

"Well, that's a surprise." Alex pulled behind a couple of cars at the red light in front of Flounder's Chowder House. He made a mental note to take Frankie there one day soon if she'd go.

"Right? She told me he was her beau. I'm floored, but they are so cute together."

A bicyclist pedaling on the sidewalk made a sudden turn and barely missed tagging a pedestrian. The woman walking pulled her earbuds out and stared after the man on the bicycle.

Alex tapped the gas and fell in behind a police car. "Where's he at now?"

"He rented a house through a vacation rental company. Looks like he'll be here for a couple of weeks."

"Wow. Better than online dating."

They shared a laugh as Alex parked in the sandy parking lot. A cool, salty breeze came from the Gulf, causing both Alex and Frankie to zip their jackets up.

After filling in a few holes and picking up a few random items left behind by beachgoers, they climbed into the truck.

"Thank you for helping me this morning."

"I appreciate the invite. To tell you the truth, I've struggled to find a purpose ever since Daddy passed away. I've been so brokenhearted." She tucked her chin low, seeming to stare at her feet. "This may seem small to you, but I felt a sense of purpose being here."

"It doesn't seem small, Frankie." The sun struck a gleam on the water as Alex searched for the right words. "Don't you see? You have a purpose. Larry made sure of that before he passed."

She cocked her head and bit her trembling lip.

His tone dropped a notch as he remembered one time Frankie had encouraged him when she was a teen. He'd been upset over an upcoming exam, and she told him he needed to pray about it. He could still remember her head full of fuzzy curls as she let him know that God would take care of him. What had happened to that little girl? "Can I ask you something?"

"Sure."

"Why don't you come to church very often?"

A sigh left her as she peered across the console at Alex. "I don't know. I just got so used to watching online, or at least that's been my excuse."

He took a Bible from the console, laying it on his lap. "Would you be open to reading some Bible verses with me?"

"Right now?"

"No better time than the present."

Her shoulders bopped slightly as a soft smile formed on her rosy lips. "Okay."

He opened the Bible halfway through and grinned. "Mama taught me that the Psalms are easily found by opening my Bible in the middle."

"I remember her teaching that in Bible class." Frankie clicked a Bible app on her iPhone.

"Let's read Psalm 121 together. I will lift up my eyes to the hills, from whence comes my help. My help comes from the Lord, Who made heaven and earth. He will not allow your foot to be moved; He who keeps you will not slumber. Behold, He who keeps Israel shall neither slumber nor sleep. The Lord is your keeper; the Lord is your shade at your right hand. The sun shall not strike you by day, nor the moon by night. The Lord shall preserve you from all evil; He shall preserve your soul. The Lord shall preserve your going out and your coming in from this time forth, and even forevermore."

Alex swallowed as memories threatened to overtake him. "Grandpa Don preached a sermon on that Psalm the month he passed away. Ever since I've studied and contemplated these words many times. The psalmist's hope didn't come from the hills but from the One who created the hills. His hope came from the Lord, the preserver of the soul."

Her lips pulled down at the corners as she let the psalm sink in. "My hope's been all over the place here lately. I've allowed my grief to rule my thoughts."

"I asked you what you were going to do about your Aunt Lottie, and you acted immediately. So, I ask you this question: what are you going to do about your hope?"

She glanced at her phone screen before anchoring her gaze on Alex. "Keatyn invited me to a Ladies' Bible study, and it starts in an hour. Can you take me home so I can get ready?"

"You bet." Alex coasted onto the highway with a smile in his heart.

Chapter 34

Even though Vandon argued she felt much bet-ter, Lottie opted to stay behind to keep an eye on her while Frankie went to the Bible study.

Lottie and Frankie had agreed to spend a few days together figuring out how to handle their new status as niece and aunt. Frankie hoped Mama would be proud of her and happy she'd connected with Lottie.

She pulled into a parking spot near the back of the lot and rushed inside. Several ladies stood in the foyer, talking and laughing. Keatyn walked up to Frankie and gave her a hug. "I spoke with Vandon a few minutes ago, and she said you were heading this way. I'm so happy you came."

Frankie returned the hug. "Me, too." She followed Keatyn and the rest of the group as they filled in the pews.

Keatyn made her way to the pulpit along with a woman who looked to be the height of an elementary school student. "Thank you all for coming this morning. It looks like we have a full house." Keatyn motioned toward the other woman. "I'm honored to introduce Nancy Donnell. She's been teaching Bible class for nearly twenty years and has been married to a preacher for just as long. Nancy and her husband, Dennis, have three beautiful children. I won't prattle on. Nancy, please come present your lesson."

Nancy settled behind the pulpit. She shuffled some papers around and smiled. "Thank you, Keatyn. She and I talked beforehand and agreed we wouldn't make any funny jokes about being married to preachers, so there goes my opening line."

She threw her right hand in the air. "Oh, well, that's probably best since Dennis always tells me my jokes about him are not very funny. Today's lesson is about love. I want to warn you all in advance I'm emotional, so overlook me if I get choked up."

"I lost my mama on June 24. Even though it'll be twenty years next year, I still remember my devastation and despair like it was yesterday. It impacted my life in so many ways that it's hard to put into words. She was my best friend, my shopping buddy, the one who went to the zoo with me before her health got too bad, and my confidant. She loved family beyond words, and it showed. Mama's passing was like a freezing cold glass of ice water thrown right in my face. It made me think about my life in comparison to hers. I thought about how she loved God and how I saw that love in her actions. Even after her passing, I saw that love. I found notes from her studies. I found letters she had written and Bible verses she would randomly write down."

She cleared her throat and took a deep breath. "I remember asking myself why I didn't love God one day."

After taking a sip of water, she paused. "I thought I loved God. I prayed regularly. I would even attend church with Mama on occasion. I remember thinking I was a good person, so surely, I would go to heaven. I was comfortable and happy with that thought."

Another pause. "Until one day, I wasn't. Until one day, I had such a strong desire to be certain I was doing God's will. It was time to put God first and love Him with my everything. Ladies, it was beyond time."

"I'm sure you've all figured it out, but today's lesson is on our love for God. And it's about to get personal. Do you love God? Truly love Him. How do you know? Have you ever searched out Bible verses on love? The pages of the Bible are full of love. God loves us beyond our comprehension, and we are told of this repeatedly."

"Do you realize that we are to love God above all else? Above friends? Above our jobs, that supports our family. Above our actual family? Above self? Yes. Above ALL else."

"Turn with me to Matthew 22 verses 37 through 39. Jesus had just been asked what the greatest commandment in the law was. Let us see how He answered. The text reads Jesus said to him, You shall love the Lord your God with all your heart, with all your soul, and with all your mind. This is the first and great commandment. And the second is like it: You shall love your neighbor as yourself."

"There's that little "all" word. These verses are clear. We are to love God with ALL our heart, soul, and mind. But what does that mean? How does God expect me to love Him? I know one thing: it means if we don't know, we better find out. Maybe you're wondering how we go about finding out."

She held up her Bible. "God has put it in black and white for us. He's given us everything we need to understand. We just have to take the time to study and to study so as to understand. We must read the Scriptures for ourselves." Nancy's lips set into a flat line, conveying how serious she was. "Do you remember the Bereans? These are people we should imitate when it comes to studying. Turn with me to Acts chapter 17, verses 10 and 11."

She flipped through the Bible in her hand. "Then the brethren immediately sent Paul and Silas away by night to Berea. When they arrived, they went into the synagogue of the Jews. These were more fair-minded than those in Thessalonica, in that they received the word with all readiness, and searched the Scriptures daily to find out whether these things were so."

"They searched the scriptures. Shouldn't we do the same, ladies? Wouldn't you agree that our soul salvation demands it? Wouldn't you also agree we should never rely on men to tell us what it takes to get to Heaven? No matter how warm and fuzzy that preacher makes you feel when he preaches on God's love, it is up to YOU to find out your part in the equation. Because you do have a part. The biggest part involves your very soul. Don't ever let anyone tell you anything different."

Frankie ran her hands along the fabric of her green sweater dress before scooting down the pew and fleeing to the ladies' room. It didn't matter if the vent blew hot air. A shiver passed over Frankie.

She hadn't studied God's love in years.

At least not with an open heart.

When she slid back into the pew beside Keatyn, she focused her attention on the speaker.

"I will never say I'm perfect or even close. I mess up. I struggle, fail, and sometimes sin, but I know Who I can turn to. I know Who will be there for me, helping me get through. He is my Rock. He is there through the good and the bad to lead me, to guide me because He loves me, and I love Him."

"Where is your love for Christ? Do you know? Do you think about Him daily? Do you set an example for your family? Your friends? Acquaintances? Do you turn to Him when things are bad? What about when things are good? Do you take the time to say thank you? To let Him know how much you appreciate and love Him? If not, now is a great time to start. I'm living my best life. The Christian life. Are you living a Christian life? If not, are you ready to live your best life? I pray you are, and you will. Reach out to me if you have questions or would like further study. I will be more than happy to study with you. Thank you, ladies, for giving me an opportunity to be here."

After a potluck luncheon, Frankie headed home with her mind on Christ and His love. She had a determination to rely on God to get her through the grief she'd been facing. She'd do better and be better.

She had to.

Chapter 35

Rhnae crossed her arms and cut a side eye at Frankie. "I can't believe we're cousins. Are you sure Lottie didn't make it up?"

"I'm sure." Frankie leaned her elbows on the picnic table. Rhnae's house parents had allowed her to meet with Rhnae in the park area beside the playground at the Children's Home. "I want to run something by you."

Her spine visibly stiffened. "I'm not living with Lottie if that's what you're wanting, don't hold your breath."

"That's not what I was going to say." Frankie blew air into her cheeks before letting it seep out. "How would you feel about living with me and Vandon?"

Her eyes narrowed as she ran her fingers over markings on the picnic table. "Seriously?"

A kid ran past them, yelling a greeting at another kid on the monkey bars. "Yes, but there are some conditions."

She made a sour face. "Isn't there always?" Her shoulders slumped like a deflated pool float. "What is it you want from me?"

"Here's the deal. I want to get to know Lottie, so if you live there, you'll be around her too."

A boy who looked to be about ten ran up behind Rhnae and pulled her ponytail. She landed a look that could curdle butter on him before putting her attention back on Frankie. "Then I guess I'll stay in this children's home forever. I won't be around a drug addict again."

"She's a recovering addict. She's been completely clean for six months."

Air huffed from Rhnae's nostrils. "Yeah, right. I'll believe it when I see it."

Frankie kept an eye on the little boy, who had apparently made a game out of pulling Rhnae's hair. "She passed a drug test."

Disbelief mixed with hope crossed her face. "What?"

"I've hired her as a full-time employee at the cabins. To keep her job, she'll have to be tested monthly."

After taking a swipe at the little boy who'd pulled her hair again, she sucked on her bottom lip for a minute. "I don't know."

Frankie never would've dreamed Rhnae would have to be convinced to leave the Children's Home.

"Rhnae, I want to get to know you, but I also want to know my mama's sister. Please give our family a chance."

Rhnae landed a hooded gaze on Frankie. "You haven't already told Lunelle and Ronnie that you're taking me home?"

"I told them I'd like to, but the decision will be up to you." Frankie held her breath. What would Rhnae say? She seemed to love a good poker face.

"It's up to me? Like, for real, my choice?"

The shock on Rhnae's face dragged a chuckle from Frankie's lips. "Absolutely."

After a few minutes of tapping her chin and having a staring contest with Frankie, Rhnae shrugged.

"I'll do it. Come stay with you, that is." The look in her eyes told Frankie she didn't think this would last. "For now."

The day had arrived to bring Rhnae home. Between Vandon, Frankie, and Lottie pacing, they'd have to replace the carpet before the day was out.

Alex poked his head through the open front door. "Hello, ladies. Frankie, you ready?"

She grabbed her purse and rocketed to where Alex waited. "We'll be back in a bit."

"We'll be waiting." Lottie's smile couldn't hide the fact that she wrung her hands like a nervous teenager on their first date. "You sure me being here won't cause any problems?"

"Positive. Rhnae asked for you to be here. I promise."

A bubble of excitement swept over Frankie as she thought of the bedroom they'd put together for Rhnae. Hopefully, Rhnae would love it.

"Are you nervous?"

"A little. Thank you for driving me. That does help with my nerves." She looked at Alex while he paid attention to the road.

Ever since the morning on the beach, they'd gotten along just fine. She'd thought or at least hoped he'd ask her out. But no such luck.

Raines had said that Brayden told Alex they were an item. He'd even used the term boyfriend. Should she say something to Alex?

Maybe he really did just look at her as a friend. He'd been silent when it came to Sierra, but Frankie hadn't noticed her coming around at all the past week.

"Not a problem. I'm glad you asked."

Frankie offered a smile but kept quiet.

Alex cleared his throat and glanced at Frankie. "I'm not dating Sierra."

Her heart nearly stopped in her chest. Had he read her mind? "Oh?" She had to play it cool.

No need to make Alex think she desperately wanted to sing and do a happy dance.

His right shoulder bobbed, and he licked his lips. "Just thought I'd tell you."

What was she supposed to say to that? Thanks? It's good to know? That makes me so happy, but now, can we get married?

HA! Married. Sometimes, her mind...well, it had a mind of its own.

In the end, she opted to keep quiet.

She couldn't trust herself to speak at the moment.

They had Rhnae and pulled into the drive at Frankie's within the hour. Alex hopped out and unloaded Rhnae's things.

Once inside, Rhnae's mouth dropped open as she spun around the open concept living and dining area. She stopped in her tracks when her eyes landed on Lottie.

Lottie stood and took a few steps closer until Rhnae held up her index finger. "You look different. Like you've gained some weight."

Lottie kept her hand wrapped around her neck. She moved her fingers every few seconds like she was massaging her throat. "I've gained a few pounds. You look good. So beautiful."

Rhnae narrowed her eyes and swallowed. "Are you really clean this time?"

Lottie nodded her head several times. Her voice hitched when she spoke. "I truly am sober, Rhnae. I've been getting drug tested, and I'll keep doing the tests weekly if I have to."

Rhnae's voice took on a less severe tone, and her eyes misted over. Her face said she desperately wanted and needed her mama to be, well, a mama. "I can see it in your face. You look pretty, Mama."

A sob left Lottie, and she held her arms out. Rhnae wasted no time bolting across the room and into her mama's arms.

Frankie motioned for Alex and Vandon to follow her onto the front porch as she fought back tears.

As soon as she stepped outside, Alex wrapped his arms around her. "I'm not sad. These are happy tears."

"You have a lot to be happy for."

"You're right. A month ago, I never would've dreamed I'd have an aunt, cousin, and house mother." She wrapped her arm in Vandon's and breathed a sigh of relief and thankfulness.

Chapter 36

October days quickly drifted to November. The Christmas Festival was on track to open with vendors, a horse-drawn carriage, and even Santa. She just wished she had Thanksgiving figured out.

Frankie, Vandon, and Rhnae had decided to travel to Des Arc for a few days to shop at the Christmas Warehouse and to see Simon. He and Vandon had been inseparable the entire time he'd stayed in Pensacola. Now that he had been home almost a week, you'd think Vandon would burst without seeing him every day.

Rhnae giggled. The excitement on her face seemed to be contagious. Her legs bounced as the airplane landed in Little Rock.

On the way to Frankie's childhood home, Rhnae gripped the passenger seat headrest from behind. "I can't believe I got to ride in an airplane. I wish Mama could see me, but I'm glad she got set up with a drug counselor."

"I take it you liked it?" Frankie asked Rhnae the question but kept her eyes on Melody. She and Frankie exchanged a smile.

Vandon let out a laugh and patted Rhnae's hand. "Looked to me like she loved it."

Frankie's bottom lip pooched out when Melody clicked the blinker to turn left as they exited the interstate in Hazen.

As soon as Melody changed direction and turned right, Frankie squealed. "Are we really stopping by Cozy Corner to grab my favorite drink?"

"I figured I didn't have much of a choice with how you've been burning a hole in my head."

Rhnae gasped and made a beeline for the purple couch when they entered Cozy Corner. Frankie grinned, a bit of buzz coursing through her own veins. Watching Rhnae experience new things brought a sense of joy to Frankie.

Drinks in hand, they climbed into Melody's car for the twenty-minute ride to Des Arc. They'd made the trip to Arkansas to shop for Christmas decorations at Guess and Company Christmas Warehouse.

Frankie had mixed feelings about going. She'd stopped truly experiencing Christmas joy and excitement after Mama passed away.

What if that joy was gone forever? How would she ever be able to pull off a Christmas Camp if she hated every second of it?

"We're here." Melody's singsong voice pulled Frankie out of the fog her mind had drifted into.

The ninety-year-old Cape Cod Cottage-style two-story home brought a flood of memories. Daddy and Mama had both loved it. The porch with seating and flowers Daddy had added for Mama, along with the dark brown shingles, gave the place more of a Tudor look.

Melody helped them unload before zipping off to meet Raines.

Rhnae let out a simple "Whoa," when they walked inside.

Vandon stopped in her tracks as she stared around the interior. Wicker furniture accented the creamy white retro sofa and black and white side chairs.

Another idea came to Frankie. She should share this place with others by turning it into a vacation rental. Ever since Guess and Company opened the Christmas Warehouse, traffic in Des Arc had gone through the roof.

Satisfied with her plan, she showed Vandon and Rhnae to their rooms before dropping her suitcase on her bed. She stopped at Daddy's room but couldn't muster up the courage to step inside. She pressed her forehead against the door as an ache threatened to consume her.

The doorbell rang, snapping her out of the melancholy attempting to overtake her. Simon grinned from ear to ear as he stepped inside. He'd promised to loan them his black Lincoln while they were in town.

Early the next morning, scents of onion and peppers coming from the kitchen greeted Frankie. Her mouth watered as she pictured Daddy around the campfire, dishing eggs from an iron skillet.

An overnight dusting of snow mixed with ice clung to the tree outside Frankie's window. The last time she'd looked out this window on such a view had been when Daddy was alive. They'd rushed outside and danced around like lunatics. The memories from that day would forever hold a special place in her heart.

She pecked on Rhnae's bedroom door. "Time to get up. Gotta get there early, and I want to show you something."

A muffled sound came from underneath the door. "Okay."

A thought struck Frankie. Daddy had always taken Mama's old potholder with them to camp. She made a beeline for the kitchen, pulling open the drawer where Daddy kept their potholders. "Morning, Vandon. Whatever you're making smells so good."

"Morning." Vandon wiped her hands down the apron she had on. "I'm making us one of your daddy's favorites from when he was a kid. A Western Omelet."

"He made one for me at camp every year until I lost interest in going with him." Frankie's hand landed on what she was looking for. Her heart tripped in her chest as she pulled out the singed light green potholder. She couldn't believe she'd forgotten about it. "Now I know where he got the recipe."

"I just hope Simon likes it."

"He will. For sure."

Frankie carried the potholder to her bedroom and slipped it inside her suitcase. No way would she leave Des Arc without it. A distant memory clouded Frankie's mind. Their first Thanksgiving after losing Mama, Daddy had cooked a Thanksgiving meal around the campfire.

Frankie's eyes doubled in size. She knew what they would do for Thanksgiving. Now, to show Rhnae how to play in the snow!

Cinnamon mixed with sugary vanilla goodness drifted through the entrance to Guess Christmas Warehouse. The fragrance washed over Frankie and took her back to the last time she spent Christmas with Mama and Daddy.

The lines of her neck worked as she forced herself to breathe. She half listened to Rhnae's excited voice before she sped through the doorway with Vandon and Simon right behind her.

Just breathe.

Melody poked Frankie's shoulder. "I'm proud of you."

Frankie's eyelids fastened shut. "Considering the fact I may not make it through the door, you better save that for later."

Melody glided past Frankie, grabbing her hand on the way by. "Nope. You're doing this, sister."

After a quick prayer for strength, Frankie picked up her pace. And stopped dead in her tracks. Colorful, sparkly nutcrackers surrounded Frankie. Her eyes darted around the space until they landed on the most beautiful nutcracker she'd ever seen. It stood tall and proud with its Christmas pink pants and red and blue sparkly shirt. Frankie's heart stuck in her throat as she locked eyes with the nutcracker.

Mama would've given anything to have him. She loved nutcrackers so much, and every year, her goal was to get one for Christmas. And Daddy never disappointed her. Maybe this nutcracker was here to help Frankie let go of her anger. Could it be?

Directly behind the nutcracker stood a massive Christmas tree filled with hot pink glittery ornaments of all shapes and sizes. Frankie couldn't believe the zings of excitement running through her veins.

Joyful laughter surrounded Frankie as she continued to walk through the Christmas Wonderland. Everywhere she looked, the nostalgia mixed with new Christmas decorations brought memories of happy times with her parents and grandparents flooding her mind. They wouldn't want Frankie to keep Christmas out of her heart forever. If she knew anything in her life, it was that.

She waved one of the young workers down. "Excuse me. I'm going to buy a lot of large items. Can I get help loading them?"

He grinned. "Yes, ma'am. That's what we're here for. We also offer shipping options if that would work better."

"That sounds perfect." She grabbed a stunned Melody's wrist. "Come on, Mel. We've got some shopping to do!"

A smile dominated her face as Christmas plans swam around her mind. She had to make this the best Christmas ever. For her parents, but also for her and the kids. They deserved a good Christmas. And maybe, just maybe, she'd get the Christmas present she'd longed for since she was thirteen.

Chapter 37

With some determination, Frankie removed the neck and giblets from inside the turkey and put them in the sink. They had a lot of cooking to do before their guests arrived for Thanksgiving dinner.

It was a good thing the kitchen had plenty of ovens and workspace to cook. After replacing the appliances and painting the walls, the main cabin looked good as new.

Rhnae's former house parents, along with a few church members who had no family and, of course, Simon, would be coming.

Alex would be flying out to Montana if he hadn't already left. Oh well. It's not like they were dating or anything, and his mama probably wanted him there with their family.

Vandon peered over her shoulder and clicked her tongue. "See, that wasn't so hard now, was it?"

Frankie made a face and stuck her tongue out. "I guess not, but I think I'd rather be outside helping Simon and Rhnae cook breakfast."

After driving the truckload of Christmas decorations and supplies here from Des Arc, Simon had decided to stay in Florida through Thanksgiving. They'd unloaded all the supplies in the storage room and had plans to put it all out the next week.

They had at least fifteen volunteers helping. Frankie's chest expanded as she bounced on her toes.

Lottie slid a cake pan into one of the ovens before smiling at Frankie. "You sound just like your mama did when she was a kid. Always wanting to be outside."

Frankie smiled as she washed her hands for the second time. "Mama always was a smart woman."

"Yes, she was." A faraway look crossed Lottie's face, and Frankie figured memories of her time with Mama had to be hard to deal with some days.

The door opened, and Rhnae yelled for them to come to eat breakfast. As they piled outside, Frankie took a moment to thank God for giving her an opportunity to get to know her family. Mama and Daddy would be proud. She had no doubt.

As soon as she stepped outside, her eyes landed on the Foster's Landscaping truck. Her heart pounded so hard it made her throat buzz. Alex held a skillet, dishing out bacon onto plates. She took the opportunity to take in every detail. The teal blue button-up shirt paired with dark-washed jeans made his eyes sparkle more than normal. As Frankie took inventory of everything Alex, she prayed he would one day feel at least a fraction of what she felt.

Seeming to sense her gaze, he looked up and grinned.

Thirty seconds earlier, she would've sworn her heart couldn't beat any faster. She would've been wrong. It seemed to demand to be felt and heard by everyone in her vicinity.

Play it cool. "I thought you were going to Montana."

He laid the skillet on one of the tables and made his way to where Frankie stood. "Nah, I didn't go."

She licked her lips, and their eyes met. "Why not?"

He scanned her face like he wanted to find something he'd lost. That made no sense, though. "Honestly, it was something Keatyn said."

"Keatyn?"

He pointed at the bench closest to the edge of the woods. "Can we talk for a minute in private?"

He'd decided to sell out. That had to be it. Why else would he want to speak to Frankie in private?

She hesitated. Would it be rude to tell him no?

Her heart and mind obviously weren't on the same page when she spoke. "Sure, what's up?"

She fell into step beside Alex as he seemed to ponder the best way to walk out of her life. That had been what she'd been trying to get him to do all along, hadn't it? Shouldn't she put the blame where it belonged?

"Frankie?"

The fog slipped out of her mind. "I'm sorry. What did you say?"

"Have a seat." He waited until she sat on the other end of the bench. His lips quirked up, and he scooted closer to Frankie. "Keatyn told me you no longer have a boyfriend."

Her neck swiveled. That was not what she'd expected him to say. "I never really had a boyfriend. I went on a few dates with Brayden, but that was it." Her eyes flickered and met his. "Why?"

Despite the comfortable, cool temperature, beads of sweat lined Alex's forehead. He licked his lips and furrowed his brow. "Do you have feelings for me, or am I imagining things?"

He may as well have sucker punched her in the gut. "Where are we going with this line of questions, Alex? Am I bothering you like when I was a kid?"

A flush crawled up his neck and cheeks. "What? No! For some reason, I'm all tongue-tied. Nothing is coming out like I want it to."

"Okay. What are you trying to say?" Her eyes bored into his as every muscle in her body went rigid.

He scooted a little closer to her, reaching out a hand to twist his fingers in her curls. "I'm in love with you." His eyes overflowed with warmth.

Her chest swelled as she caught her breath. She looked up and met the eyes of what looked to be the same little bird that had kept coming around the past few weeks. But this time, it perched on the limb, watching her and Alex.

Did birds people watch? What a ridiculous thing to think about. Alex just said what she'd prayed for and longed for almost half her life. She needed to say something meaningful and smart.

But did that happen? Not at all. Instead, a big goofy grin lined her face. "Remember me telling you about that Halloween movie with the guy who reminded me of you?"

He paused for a moment before tilting his head to the side. "Um, yeah, I think so."

"Well, I left out the part where he saved the girl from getting murdered, and I always imagined he was you, and I was the girl."

A lop-sided grin twitched his lips and reached his eyes. "You wanted me to save you from getting murdered?"

She giggled and shook her head as she closed the space between them. "No, silly. I wanted you to love me enough *to* save me from getting murdered."

A laugh broke from his chest. "You're something else, Frances Kingston."

"Just shut up and kiss me."

"Yes, ma'am." He reached around Frankie and pulled her face close to his.

She put her finger up to his mouth and grinned. "I forgot to say I love you, too." She removed her finger and met his eyes. "Now, you can kiss me."

Her heart doubled in speed, even more than it had earlier, as she shared a kiss with Alex for the second time in her life.

Oh, and having him as a willing participant this time made the kiss that much sweeter.

Chapter 38

The Christmas tree had always gone up the day after Thanksgiving before Mama passed away. That tradition seemed to scream to be reinstated at the cabins this year.

A Christmas song by Kelly Clarkson wafted through the outdoor air as Frankie took everything in. Alex had found a tree almost as big as his truck and set it up in the grassy area at the front of the cabin. Several kids from the Children's Home buzzed around the massive tree, each one adding an ornament here and there along the way.

On one side of the yard, Lottie and Vandon worked a hot cocoa stand while Cordelia and Keatyn passed out candy canes. Across from them, Gareth and another man from church roasted nuts.

They had at least fifteen volunteers helping. Frankie's chest expanded as she bounced on her toes. This is what Daddy had wanted. He wanted

Frankie to find a bit of joy and maybe even some of the Christmas spirit she'd lost after Mama passed.

As darkness fell, Alex came out of the cabin, heading in her direction. Frankie's breathing soared into high gear and got even worse when he stopped by her side.

"This is great, Frankie." His fingers trailed down her palm, leaving tingles behind. "Larry would be so proud."

She searched his eyes. "Do you really think so?"

"I do." Alex scanned the place like he needed another look to know what to say. "He had big dreams for this place and for you."

"I just want to live up to his expectations." Frankie focused on a large red bell ornament one of the kids hung on the tree. Anything to keep from looking at Alex. Right now, she'd probably cry, and that's not what she wanted to do. She wanted to be happy. Merry, even.

Alex tugged on her hand until she met his gaze. "As long as you put God first and do everything in your power to do His will, you'll more than live up to Larry's expectations."

"I promise I'm going to try."

"That's all anyone can do. Try." He leaned his forehead to hers for a second before stepping away with a smile. "Can I buy you some roasted nuts or hot cocoa?"

Frankie grinned. "It's all free, silly."

The volunteers had brought the food, and Lottie had also gotten several local businesses to donate some of what they needed. It turned out Lottie had a way of helping people see the need to donate their time and money.

Laughter from the kids echoed through the air, mixing with another Christmas song. Daddy had been right – these kids deserved to be happy.

Alvin Griffin pulled up in a tractor-trailer with a load of hay. Frankie's mouth fell open, and she cocked her head at Alex. "What's this?"

He kissed her hand, setting her hand and heart on fire. "I wanted to surprise you. How about we get that cocoa and take a ride?"

Several people formed a line, waiting for Alvin to give the go-ahead to get on the hay.

Rhnae walked by, making goo-goo eyes at a boy who looked to be about sixteen. They got in line for the ride, seeming to be lost in their own world.

Frankie grabbed Alex's hand as she started toward the line. "Let's skip the cocoa for now."

There's no way she'd allow Rhnae to be alone with a boy like this. Nope.

Alex followed her line of sight and shook his head. "Okay, ride first, cocoa later."

After the ride, Frankie glanced at her watch. "We need to start the tree lighting ceremony."

"Sounds good." He nodded toward Rhnae and raised a brow. "Rhnae and the young man kept a respectable space between them during the ride."

"Did they?" Frankie screwed her lips up and shrugged. "I didn't notice."

He leaned close to Frankie. "Liar."

She feigned shock. "Well, I never!"

Alex cleared his throat. "Who's ready to see the tree lit?"

Applause came from the crowd as Frankie pointed at Rhnae. "Rhnae, would you like to do the honors?"

Rhnae squealed as she dashed to where Frankie stood and grasped the switch. They started a countdown, and as soon as they reached one, Rhnae clicked the switch. Green, red, gold and blue lights flashed to life. Everyone clapped, and a few even yelled Merry Christmas.

Franke grinned. Merry Christmas, indeed.

Chapter 39

The arrival of December brought a childlike joy to Alex. Maybe the fact that he and Frankie had finally talked about their feelings played a big part in it.

He clipped the last bit of lights on the cabin and smiled at his handiwork. Frankie was going to love the colorful display.

"Hey, let's finalize the name of the camp real quick."

Alex smiled within himself as he climbed down the ladder. She wouldn't know what real quick was if it knocked her on the head. They'd been working on a name for the new retreat for days now, to no avail.

He entered the conference room and joined Simon and Vandon at the table. Frankie remained standing as she opened a notebook.

"Last time we met, we couldn't agree on a final name for the retreat." She glanced at Vandon, and her lips lifted at the corners. "Vandon voted to name it after Lake Loblolly."

Vandon leaned back in her chair, almost bumping the wall. "Yep, but Simon and Alex said they didn't think that name sounded very retreaty."

"Right. If we're planning to host wellness retreats, youth camps, Bible camps, school events...etc. then we need a more universal name."

"I take it you have some ideas?"

"Actually, Rhnae did some research and put this together for us." Frankie tapped the notebook before glancing at her watch. "Lottie texted that they were almost here a few minutes ago. She's letting Rhnae drive home from school."

Right on cue, two car doors slammed. Within minutes, Rhnae dropped her backpack on the table and popped her hand on her hip. "Mama accused me of trying to kill her."

Lottie trudged in behind her and fell into the wall. Dreamy, the cat followed her, looking at her like she was crazy.

Lottie threw her hand over her face and cried out like she was in pain. "Somebody save me from this child's driving!" The smile that brightened her face gave away the fact that she was just giving Rhnae a hard time.

Rhnae rolled her eyes and bunched her mouth up. "You are so dramatic. My driving is fine." She glanced at Frankie and jumped up and down a few times. "Is that my notebook?"

Frankie's lips twitched into a grin. "It is. I want you to tell everyone your thoughts on the name."

Rhnae's face turned serious as she took the notebook. "Well, I understand your desire to reference Loblolly Lake when naming the cabins. So, I decided to do some research on the Loblolly pine tree."

She flipped the page on the notebook before laying it on the table. "The Loblolly pine was taken aboard the Apollo 14 flight to the moon, and the seeds were planted in different parts of the United States afterward. Is that not cool?"

"Yes, that is cool." Vandon grinned.

Lottie couldn't have looked prouder if Rhnae had just told her she'd been elected President of the United States.

"Since the tree is so cool and the lake is already named after it, we should kinda name it the same but different. I found some other names for the Loblolly Pine." She tucked a chunk of blonde hair behind her ear and grinned. "How about Rosemary Pines Retreat?"

"That couldn't be more perfect, Rhnae," Both Frankie and Vandon said at the same time.

Simon chuckled. "If you lived closer, I'd hire you at my Law Firm. Good job." He entwined his hand with Vandon's and looked around the room. "Now that that's settled, we have some news."

Pink splotches appeared on Vandon's cheeks, giving her a youthful glow Alex had never seen before. "We're engaged."

Lottie squealed.

Rhnae gasped.

Frankie looked like she'd seen a ghost. Alex wasn't sure if she would congratulate them or pass out.

Chapter 40

In the end, Frankie congratulated Vandon and Simon. As soon as the meeting ended, she started making phone calls. This wedding had to be perfect. Vandon insisted they not make a fuss. Said they had enough going on preparing for the Christmas festival, but Frankie refused to listen.

Not only was it Vandon's day, but it would also be the first official event at Rosemary Pines Retreat. Luckily, the owner of VIP Creations, from Des Arc, agreed to fly in and stay on staff until the wedding. Frankie had known Effie Clairday for a few years, and she put on the best weddings ever.

Frankie scanned the area, and a sharp zing snapped her insides at the beauty. This place screamed Christmas with a capital C. Booths lined the entire walkway closest to the entrance. A lot of local vendors would be there, and some of the kids had crafts to sell. They'd even mapped off a trail for carriage rides.

Frankie moved the guest book Effie had made from a cutting board over an inch or so and stepped back. Perfect.

She glanced at the chairs. Vandon had asked to cover them in a light blue, and flower bouquets made from old hymnals were attached to the chair at the end of each aisle. If Frankie ever got married, she'd use VIP Creations. She'd never figure out how people made such stunning arrangements out of paper.

Simon and Vandon opted to keep the guest list at thirty people so their wedding would be more intimate. Guests had started filling the seats when Frankie's vision locked on Alex. He had on a tuxedo. Wow. Her legs went wobbly, and she had to focus on breathing.

Simon touched her elbow. "Frankie. Thank you for doing this."

She forced herself to look at Simon instead of Alex. "You're very welcome. I've truly enjoyed it."

"You remember the day I told you Larry asked you to move to Pensacola for a reason?"

"I sure do. I was so upset that day trying to deal with losing Daddy and then wondering why he'd put this burden on me."

"Remember I told you I think Larry did this for a reason? How do you feel about it now?"

"I think you were right. Daddy knew what he was doing. Now, having Alex as a partner threw me for a loop."

A bark of laughter came from Simon. "You don't seem to mind so much now."

Heat kissed her cheeks. "I don't mind at all, and I know Alex was the second person in line for the place if I said no."

Simon shrugged. "Awe, it doesn't matter now. Does it?"

Her eyes followed Alex as he disappeared into the cabin. Effie cleared her throat a couple of times. Frankie shifted her gaze to Effie as she gave her the thumbs up. The wedding was about to start. "Not at all, Simon."

Alex and Vandon made a striking picture as she held onto his arm. Her light pink pantsuit stood out next to his dark tuxedo. Simon looked so happy. So did Vandon. Lottie and Rhnae sat together while Frankie stood next to Simon. One glance at Alex and her heart tripped over itself.

Yeah, Daddy knew exactly what he was doing.

A local band called Mustang Dreams took the stage and started playing Jingle Bells as people bustled around the Christmas Festival. Frankie bobbed her head along to the tune and blew a kiss at her phone screen. "Love you, Mel and Raines. I can't wait to meet that baby! Oh, and Mel, try not to do too much until he or she is born."

Alex popped up behind Frankie and waved at the camera. "Congratulations, guys. I hope you get to feeling better, Melody."

"Thanks, you two. The festival looks great, and I see lots of people. Maybe next year we can be there with the new baby."

"I hope so." One of the vendors waved Alex over, so he said his goodbyes and jogged up to the booth.

Melody yawned and pressed her head into the pillow. "I love you and can't wait to see you, Frankie, but I gotta get some rest."

"Love you, too." She blew a kiss before ending the call.

She slipped her phone into her back pocket and took her time watching everyone and everything. She headed toward the booths, looking for a brownie or something sweet.

Rhnae ran up and gave Frankie a high five. "I don't know if I've told you this, but I'm so glad you're my cousin."

Frankie grinned and pulled Rhnae in a bear hug. "Me, too." She looked up and traded a glance with Lottie. Lottie rubbed her favorite cat, Dreamy, as she landed a sweet smile on Frankie just like Mama used to.

Vandon stepped on the stage and cleared her throat. "May I have your attention, please? It's time for our Ugly Christmas Sweater contest results. I need our top three finalists to join me on stage."

Rhnae's former house mother, Lunelle, a twelve- or thirteen-year-old girl named Savannah from the Children's Home, and a man Frankie didn't recognize took the stage beside Vandon. Lunelle had what looked like real deer horns pinned all over a camouflage sweatshirt overlaid with a string of blinking lights. Savannah had a teddy bear pinned to a red sweater wrapped up in green blinking lights. The man had a donkey pulling a sleigh with homemade multi-color bows tied all around a black sweatshirt.

Vandon pointed to the drummer and grinned. "Can I get a drumroll, please?"

The drummer obliged and started the countdown. Vandon opened a card shaped like a Christmas present. "And the winner of the first-ever Rosemary Pines Ugly Christmas sweater contest is Savannah Moore!"

Savannah jumped up and down and squealed as Vandon handed her an envelope with a check for twenty-five dollars inside.

Frankie headed to the lake for a moment to think and pray as the festivities wound down for the night. A cool breeze hit her face and reminded her of the fall at Lake Des Arc.

"You up for some company?" Alex stopped a few feet away from the edge of the lake.

"I'm always up for your company." Alex closed the space between them, and she snuggled close to his chest.

He chuckled. "So, no more laser lights, or... what kind of fruit was it that smelled like death?"

She playfully punched his side. "Am I ever going to live that down?"

"Never." He rubbed the back of his neck and winced. "As long as you don't pull out your taser, I won't mind the rest so much. Well, except for the fruit."

A hearty laugh left her chest. "Mrs. Pinkerton would probably run me out of town if I brought that fruit back."

He brushed his hand across her cheek, and his voice turned husky. "I'd follow you anywhere, woman."

She sank her face into his hand and breathed in the spicy goodness she'd come to know as Alex Foster. "You better."

Epilogue

The past year had been the busiest year of Frankie's life. Rosemary Pines Retreat had hosted a Bible Camp, a couple of weddings, a work retreat, and now the second annual Christmas Festival.

She had made herself right with the Lord and had a happiness she couldn't describe. Attending service was no longer a hardship. It was an act of love. Maybe this is the feeling that Daddy always talked to her about.

Simon and Vandon split their time between Des Arc and Pensacola. Arkansas was their home in the summer and Florida for the winter months. They decided they were turning into snowbirds, and both declared they wouldn't have it any other way.

Frankie rubbed her hands down her red slacks and took a deep breath. The local news station had just pulled up to cover the festival's opening night.

Frankie waved at the reporter before she glanced around, allowing her eyes to linger on each section of the festival. Alex had installed lights all over the place. It reminded Frankie of a scene from a Christmas movie. Magical!

Mustang Dreams, the same band from the year before, belted out Holly Jolly Christmas as people strolled along. A few ladies had stopped in front of the stage, clapping along to the music.

This year, they'd added a couple of tents to go along with the booths. One tent housed a lesson on crafting for Christmas hosted by a lady from church named Rebecca VanHouten, and their former contractor and new church member, Clarence Little, had a section on building things for Christmas. They had another tent with a local chef named Baxter Bond, who volunteered to teach people how to make the perfect Christmas dessert. Both tents had people lined up to get inside.

One of Frankie's favorite things they added happened to be the Snow Globe Photo Booth. Based on the line of people waiting to get inside, she decided she wasn't the only one who loved it.

The vendor booths bustled with customers and people waiting for Santa Claus to make his appearance. Savannah Moore had a vendor booth filled with homemade ugly Christmas sweaters. Frankie grinned as she stopped at the booth.

Savannah tucked a chunk of strawberry blonde hair behind her ear and lifted her mouth into a smile. "Hi, Frankie!"

"Hi there. I'm impressed with what you've done with the sweaters. They're so original, and I bet you make a ton of money."

Savannah beamed at the compliment. "Thank you so much."

After saying their goodbyes, Frankie moved out of the way of several customers. Applause mixed with laughter and squeals of delight pricked Frankie's ears, and she smiled to herself.

When she stopped at Lottie's booth, gingerbread and sugar cookies invaded Frankie's senses, making her stomach growl. "I'll be shocked if you don't sell out tonight. All this looks and smells so good."

Lottie grinned as she replaced a stack of cookies on one of the empty trays. "I sure hope so."

Rhnae's voice broke through the crowd as she carted a few more pans of goodies. "Excuse me. Coming through with warm and delicious baked goods."

Keatyn called out a greeting as she and Gareth strolled by with their little girl, Lily. Cordelia and Myles Griffin waved as they worked to keep up with Lily. Everyone Frankie knew had come out to show their support.

Even Alex's family had flown in from Montana. His mama had been tickled when she found out they were dating. Frankie's heart swelled in her chest as she exchanged hellos with passersby.

Vandon and Simon pushed a stroller up to Frankie and stopped. Simon rested his hand on Vandon's back and leveled a look of love at her the same as he did the day they married. "Look at this precious little boy."

Frankie leaned into the stroller and rubbed little Roy's hand. "Where's Melody and Raines? Or did you hijack the baby?"

"Oh, they're taking a carriage ride." A cheeky smile crossed Vandon's face. "And yes, I hijacked this sweet little thing, but I don't think they minded."

Frankie scanned the area. "Have either of you seen Alex?"

Vandon shrugged. "Surely, he's around here somewhere. Have you checked the bench by the lake?"

"I think that would be a good spot to check," Simon said.

"Okay. I'll check there." She glanced in that direction. "I wanted him to be here when Santa comes."

Christmas lights lit the path to the lake, and whiffs of peppermint seemed to come out of nowhere. Thanks to Guess and Company, this truly had turned out to be a Christmas Wonderland.

She came to a fast halt when she got close to the lake. What in the world was Santa Claus doing out here? "Hey. Shouldn't you be on the carriage by now?"

When she got no response, she marched around the bench, stopping in front of him. She opened her mouth to ask the same question but stopped when green eyes met hers. "Santa Claus heard you've been a good girl this year."

She had to admit that the past year with Alex had not been boring. She nodded and landed the most serious look she could muster on him. "Santa Claus heard right."

"Santa Claus thinks you deserve something nice and sparkly on this Christmas Eve." He dropped to one knee and opened a red box he'd been hiding on his lap.

A single round diamond on a gold band sparkled on top of red velvet.

He tore off the Santa hat and met her misty gaze. "Frankie, when I was eighteen, I never would've thought you were the one for me, but I believe God had a plan for us. A plan that would take some time and a lot of patience." A grin split his face. "I have a question for you. One I've wanted to know the answer to for a very long time."

A sob pricked her chest, and she fell to her knees in front of Alex. "Yes, the answer is yes!"

At the same time, Alex asked, "Are eyebrows also considered facial hair?"

Her tears gave way to an abrupt laugh. Yes, she'd never be bored as long as he was around.

He joined her in laughter for a few seconds before his face became serious. His Adam's apple moved as he swallowed. "I love you dearly and can't imagine life without you as my wife. Will you do me the honor of marrying me?"

"I knew you were my husband way before you knew I was your wife, remember?" She stuck her ring finger out. "So, there's no way I'd say no to the offer I've waited for since I was thirteen years old. I love you so much."

He slipped the ring on her finger before twirling her around and planting a kiss on her lips. "Wanna join me on the carriage, Mrs. Claus?"

She looked at her loose jeans and zebra print sweater. "I'm not really dressed for that."

Melody came out of nowhere and handed Frankie a red cape lined with white fur. "I've got you covered, Mrs. Claus."

The look on Alex's face sent her blood into a tizzy as she slipped the robe on. "You once said you'd follow me anywhere. Well, I'd do the same for you, Santa."

Thank you for taking the time to read **Frankie's Journey**. If you found it enjoyable, I would be grateful if you could leave a review. Your feedback truly makes a difference!

Acknowledgements

Writing the third book in our Seeds of Faith series has been so much fun. My grandma, Frankie, was a hoot, so getting to honor her life has brought me many smiles.

Carissa - you brought our fictional Frankie to life for me. You're beautiful both inside and out, and I'm thankful you're my daughter!

Shelby with SMB Photography captured an amazing shot that flows perfectly on the cover. Thank you, Shelby!

Thank you to Paul for allowing me to tour your beautiful Christmas Warehouse, to include it in the book, and to use it as inspiration!

Ashley – I appreciate you for bringing me into The Lily Pad, allowing me to sell books there, and giving Frankie a place to work while she lived in Des Arc.

To Jill at Cozy Corner Nutrition – I'm happy Frankie had a cool place to enjoy her favorite drinks.

To my ARC readers, thank you a million times for reading my stories and giving feedback.

Thank you to Vickie M. for reading as I wrote and giving great feedback.

My honey, Mark, is such a gem for continuing to grant me full access to his library of sermons. He preaches from the heart, and I'm so glad he's mine!

To the person who proofread, edited, and provided such fantastic feedback, WOW! Dear Stephanie, your comments made me laugh (and cry, haha), but you always make my stories flow so much better!

If I've left anyone out, just know it's because I'm forgetful and mean no disrespect!

Dear readers, thank you from the bottom of my heart. I appreciate your support! Please stay tuned as we continue this series with even more journeys.

XOXO

About the Author

Leah Brewer is a multi-genre author who focuses on writing clean books that anyone can read. She is a Writers Ink of Northeast Arkansas member and is currently working on a murder mystery.

Leah was born and raised in Des Arc, Arkansas, before moving to Northeast Arkansas when her children were young. Growing up, you could find Leah playing make-believe near the White River or as she waded through water deep in the woods.

She spends her spare time with her husband, Mark, their grown children, and their new granddaughter, Charlotte. If she's not on a beach, she's dreaming about when she can be!